THE SCHEME FOR
FULL EMPLOYMENT

Also by Magnus Mills

The Restraint of Beasts

Only When the Sun Shines Brightly (stories)

All Quiet on the Orient Express

Three to See the King

THE SCHEME FOR
FULL EMPLOYMENT

Magnus Mills

Picador USA
New York

www.picadorusa.com

Picador® is a U.S. registered trademark and is used by St. Martin's Press under license from Pan Books limited.

Library of Congress Cataloging-in-Publication Data
Mills, Magnus.
    The scheme for full employment / Magnus Mills.—1st Picador USA ed.
    p.cm
    ISBN 0-312-42163-X
    1. Full employment policies—Fiction. 2. Labor policy—Fiction.
    I. Title.

PR6063.J37784 S34 2002
823'.914—dc21

                                              2002035492

First published in Great Britain by Flamingo, an imprint of
HarperCollins*Publishers*

First Picador USA Edition: December 2002

10 9 8 7 6 5 4 3 2 1

For my father

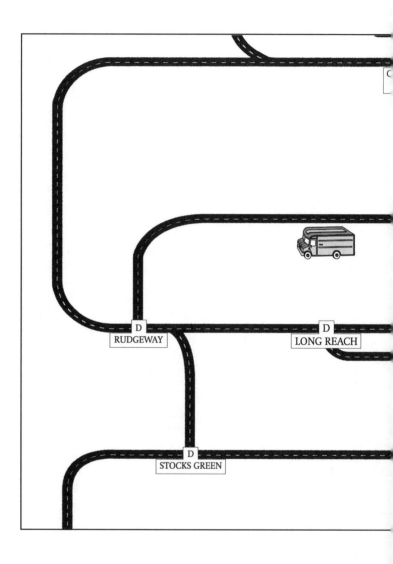

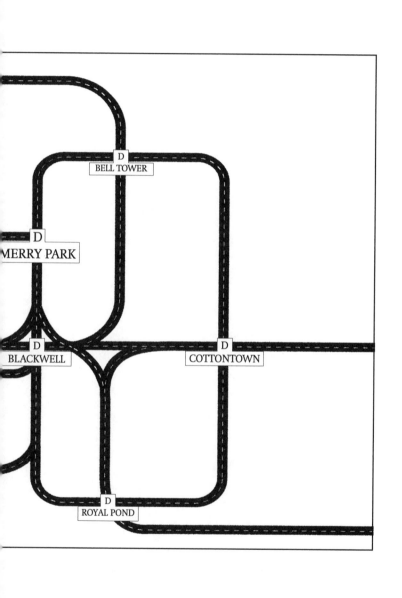

SAMPLE DUTY (for training purposes only) Leaflet T12

Start/finish Long Reach depot.

8.00 Collect Keys.

8.02 Attend vehicle during loading/unloading.

8.15 Depart Long Reach depot and proceed east along Ring Road.

10.15 Arrive Cotton Town depot. Attend vehicle during loading/unloading.

11.00 Depart Cotton Town depot and proceed north. (note: observe 20mph speed limit along Butler's Causeway.)

12.45 Arrive Bell Tower depot. Attend vehicle during loading/unloading.

13.00 Dinner break.

13.30 Attend vehicle during loading/unloading.

13.45 Depart Bell Tower depot and proceed west. (note: during diversions, drivers should be aware of low bridge at New Borough Sidings. Normal cautions apply.)

15.00 Arrive Rudgeway depot. (Enter via Rudgeway Approach, not rear gate.) Attend vehicle during loading/unloading.

15.45 Depart Rudgeway depot.

16.20 Arrive Long Reach depot. Secure vehicle and return keys.

16.30 End of duty.

(All journeys subject to curtailment or rerouting as exigencies dictate.)

Of course, if this had been any other country The Scheme would still be going today. In any other country it would have been regarded as a national treasure, with the entire workforce striving to maintain the high standards and principles on which it was established. As a matter of fact, many of our continental neighbours adopted versions of The Scheme for their own use, and in each case they achieved unbounded success. Yet there's no question whose idea it was in the first place. It was ours. We thought it up. The Scheme for Full Employment was the envy of the world: the greatest undertaking ever conceived by men and women. It solved at a stroke the problem that had beset humankind for generations. Participants had only to put the wheels in motion, and they could look forward to a bright, sunlit upland where idleness and uncertainty would be banished for ever. Planned to the finest detail by people of vision, The Scheme was watertight, and could not possibly go wrong.

Except in this country.

In this country we managed to destroy it. We destroyed the last thing that could save us from obscurity and ruin. And we did it with our own hands too, not at the behest of some errant leader whom we could obey and then blame later. No, we can't lay the guilt on anyone but ourselves. The Scheme was created for us, and it was we who finally brought it down.

THE SCHEME FOR
FULL EMPLOYMENT

I

Len Walker saw the dangers long before the rest of us. I remember a conversation we had one morning as we stood on the loading bay at Blackwell depot, watching the UniVans roll in and out of the yard. It was a fine day, the first after a long damp spell, and several drivers were treating their vehicles to a trip through the automatic wash. At the same time goods were being cleared from the bay as quickly as they came in, with not an item of clutter in sight. It was a hive of activity, and I remarked that everything appeared to be running smooth as clockwork.

'Oh yes,' said Len. 'It all looks very rosy, but you know it could easily come to an end, don't you?'

'Come to an end?' I said. 'Surely not.'

'It could happen overnight.'

'But you always say we're living in glorious days.'

'Certainly we are! Glorious, glorious days!'

'Well then.'

'Well then nothing.' Len lowered his voice. 'These may be glorious days, but if we lose them they'll never come again.'

'Why should we lose them?'

'Because some people have started taking too much for granted. Too many liberties, if you get my meaning. I'm not naming names, but there are a few individuals around here threatening to undermine everything that's been built up over the years. They don't seem to realize it could collapse like a house of cards if they're not careful.'

'Really?'

'Oh, it may not happen for a while yet, and I'm sure we'll be able to continue just as we are for quite some time. Nonetheless, if we're overcomplacent, if we fail to cherish what we have, then I tell you, one morning we'll wake up and find it gone.'

'Have you mentioned this to anyone else?'

'Only those who'll listen. There are a number of us scattered about, spreading the word, so to speak. Obviously it's a slow process, getting through to everybody, trying to make them fully aware of the situation. Not everyone's as conscientious as you and me.'

'Well, I wouldn't say I was particularly conscientious. I like an easy time, same as the next person.'

'Maybe so,' Len replied. 'But I can see you appreciate The Scheme more than most of them.'

'Possibly.'

'Not so sure about your assistant though.'

'George? No, I don't think he ever considers such matters. More interested in distributing his cakes than anything else.'

'Well, do me a favour, will you? Try and drum the message into him and all those others who just drift along thinking this'll last for evermore. Otherwise, ten years from now they'll come back here and find the gates locked and trees growing up through the concrete.'

'Alright, I'll try my best. Look, Len, I'd better get going. Osgood's peeping out. I'll catch you next time round, OK?'

'Yes. See you.'

He moved aside and watched as I descended the steps and walked to the front of the UniVan. He was still watching when I climbed inside, and I got the feeling he was observing me to see whether his words had sunk in properly.

I slid the cab door shut. George was sitting in the dummy seat, surrounded by a stack of pink and white boxes.

'You been here all the while?' I said. 'I thought you were going to see Osgood.'

'No,' he replied. 'I've decided to leave it for the moment. It's going to require careful timing.'

'Suit yourself. You ready to go then?'

'Yep.'

'Right, let's move.'

I started up and headed across the yard and out through the gates.

'What were you and Len talking about?' George asked, raising his voice above the engine. 'You've been rabbiting on for ages.'

'Well, you know what he's like once he gets going.'

'Yeah . . .'

'He's been telling me how The Scheme's likely to fizzle out of existence at any minute.'

'He's changed his tune. Last time I spoke to him he told me we'd never had it so good.'

'Oh, he still believes all that,' I said. 'But he thinks no one else does. Apart from a select few.'

'What, like him and Mick Dalston when they're up in the games room for hours on end? Keeping it spick and span, as they put it.'

'Exactly.'

'So what's his problem then?'

'Well, you know Len takes his breakfast, dinner and tea breaks all rolled together into one?'

'Yeah,' said George. 'Has done for years.'

'But despite that he always keeps on top of the work, doesn't he?'

'Suppose.'

'And when was the last time you saw a muddle on the bay at Blackwell?'

'Can't remember.'

'Well, I can. It was when Len had his summer holiday and Charlie Green took over for two weeks.'

'Oh, that's right.'

'And Charlie kept going on about how Gosling was good for the clock if you leant on him a bit. Got himself signed out early three days in succession, and by the time Len came back there was enough backlog to make several loads.'

'He got quite upset about that, didn't he?'

'I'll say he did. Went up the wall, as a matter of fact. Didn't speak to Charlie for several months. The point I'm making is that Len always does his full eight hours even though he spends half of them upstairs. He never clocks off early because he doesn't want to jeopardize his darts, and his cards, and his snooker, and all the other leagues he's running. He's been on The Scheme a long time, don't forget. He wants it all to stay exactly as it is, but he's afraid it could crumble into nothing.'

'Why should it?'

'Because none of us values it enough.'

'Oh, he hasn't got to worry about that,' declared George. 'Lenny's trouble is he takes it all too seriously.'

'You sure about that?'

'Course I'm sure. Look, you know as well as I do The Scheme's unsinkable. These UniVans were purpose-built for the task, weren't they? Thousands of them, specially designed with interchangeable parts and immunity to rust. They'll go for years and years if they're looked after properly, and as long as they've got a future, then so have we. Nobody in their right mind's going to take them off the road. There'd be a public out-cry if they did, and besides, what would become of all the depots, and the service plants, and the ancillaries?

They're no use for anything else. Trust me, we won't get closed down just because Charlie Green works an early swerve from time to time.'

'Well, I hope you're right,' I said. 'If only for Len's sake.'

While we'd been talking we'd got onto the Ring Road and were now heading east. Every so often we encountered UniVans coming the other way, and if they were from Long Reach we gave them a flash with our headlights. (If they originated from other depots we ignored them.) We'd already said hello in this manner to Dave Whelan and Mick Clark, followed shortly afterwards by John Ford and Colin Regis. A minute later we ran into a spot of heavy traffic, and I had to slow down to just above walking speed.

'Changing the subject,' said George. 'You know I'm off the next two weeks, don't you?'

'Yeah,' I said. 'I saw the holiday list.'

'Oh, right. Will you be OK for the cakes then?'

I turned to him. 'What?'

'The cakes.'

'Yes,' I said. 'I know the cakes. I meant: what do you mean "the cakes"?'

'Well, can you do them?'

'Course I can't do them.'

'Why not?'

'Because they're your cakes, George. I don't mind you bringing them on the runs when you're here. That's one thing. But I'm not lugging them round while you swan off on holiday.'

'There'll only be a few.'

'I don't care; I'm not doing them.'

'But Trace'll kill me.'

'That's between you and Trace,' I said. 'The Scheme doesn't exist for your girlfriend's personal benefit, you know.'

'I'm aware of that,' said George. 'But, come on, as a favour to me. You know I'll see you alright.'

Suddenly something dawned on me. 'This is why you put off seeing Osgood this morning, isn't it? You've got to ask him as well.'

George sighed. 'Yeah. Look, mate, I could really do with your help on this one. I know she pushes it a bit sometimes, but when you've got a job like ours you have to make the most of it, don't you?'

'If you say so.'

'And you won't need do them Wednesday.'

'Why, what's Wednesday?'

'February 29th.'

'So?'

'Leap year, isn't it? There's no birthdays. Not round here, anyway.'

'Well, that's something to celebrate,' I said. 'Hello, what are they up to?'

Waiting to emerge from a junction just ahead of us was a UniVan containing the two Steves. Actually, I could only see Steve Moore from this angle. He was behind the wheel as usual, but I knew that the person lost from view in the dummy seat would be Steve Armstrong. What caught my attention, though, was the way the vehicle was being driven, which struck me as slightly out of character. Rather than forcing his way into the line of traffic, in the manner typical of most drivers on The Scheme, Steve was politely holding back, waiting for a space to appear. None did, of course, as nobody wanted to get stuck behind a UniVan if they could avoid doing so. It would be up to me to let him in, and as we drew nearer I flashed the lights and waited for some sort of acknowledgement. Instead, without even a glance in our direction, he simply pulled forward into the gap I'd left him, and then went straight across the junction and up the road opposite! At the same moment I realized that he was quite alone in his cab. Steve Armstrong was nowhere to be seen.

'Who does he think he is?' I cried. 'Cutting across there like that!'

'Dunno,' said George. 'Bit dodgy coming off the authorized, isn't it? I thought he and Steve were supposed to be on twenty-two.'

'So did I! See the way he just cruised in front of us without so much as a nod?'

I had to admit I was rattled by the sight of Steve Moore gaily sailing along an unauthorized route, enjoying the freedom of the road and doing so completely on his own. As far as I knew this was unheard of. In all the time I'd been on The Scheme I'd only ever had a UniVan to myself when we were parked up and George was off performing one of his many private errands. To drive without an accompanying assistant was prohibited, and having seen Steve doing just that made me feel quite envious. How, I wondered, did he think he would get away with it at eleven o'clock in the morning, in broad daylight?

'He'll get booked if he carries on like that,' remarked George.

'Yes,' I agreed. 'Let's hope he does.'

We watched as Steve's vehicle gradually disappeared into the hinterland of side streets, industrial premises and warehouses that lay to the south of the Ring Road. Then, without further speculation, we continued on our way. We were due to arrive at Cotton Town depot at twelve forty-five, but as usual by mid-morning we were well ahead of schedule. This didn't bother us, though, as we had an extra call to make. After another two miles I pulled up beside a parade of shops, and George clambered out with his stack of cake boxes.

'Do you want to come and say hello to Sandro?' he asked. 'So you're clued up for next week?'

'You've decided I'm doing them after all then, have you?'

'Oh come on, mate. I thought you'd agreed.'

'Alright, but you'd better bring me back a stick of rock.'

'Where from?'

'The seaside.'

'I'm not going to the seaside in February, am I?'

'Where are you going then?'

'Nowhere.'

'Well, you can still get me a stick of rock,' I said. 'It'll give you something interesting to do while you're off work.'

'Thanks, pal.'

Strictly speaking it was a bookable offence to leave the vehicle unattended, but nearly everyone did it these days so I switched off and we went to Sandro's Bakery, taking care to leave the cab doors shut. We'd had the heater switched on since ten to eight that morning and we didn't want to lose the warmth so carefully accumulated. The fiery blast that hit us when we entered the kitchen, however, made us wonder why we'd bothered.

'Blimey,' I murmured as George ushered me inside. 'Imagine having to work in this heat all the time.'

I had in fact met Sandro on one former occasion when Trace saddled George with so many cakes that I'd had to help him carry them all in. He appeared to have forgotten this, however, and it was easier for the two of us to be introduced afresh. In truth, there was only time for a quick handshake and exchange of greetings because Sandro and his assistants were rushing round like madmen, each apparently performing several tasks at once, just as they had been on my previous visit. This call was really just so that Sandro would know me when I turned up with the cakes next week, but when we departed a few minutes later I had a large bagful of doughnuts in my hand, presented as a gesture of goodwill. This made it quite worthwhile. We sat in the cab and ate half of them, and I decided that helping George out wasn't going to be such a hardship after all.

We'd also collected one additional box from the bakery. This contained the cake that George hoped to leave overnight in Osgood's office. It had received its coat of icing and was now ready for the next stage in its journey, namely, to be passed into the hands of Pete Giggs.

'How long's Pete got left on run seven?' I asked, as George carefully placed the cake on top of the dashboard.

'Finishes end of next week,' he replied. 'Then he goes onto fourteen.'

'So he'll be no use to you for a while after that.'

'It's not a question of use,' George protested. 'It's a mutual arrangement. I help him with his bits and pieces. He helps me with mine.'

'Osgood's not going to be so easy though.'

'Well, he was alright last time I asked him. Should be OK if I handle him carefully. I think I'll have to regard this as a test case.'

By the time we got moving again it was comfortably past twelve o'clock, so we enjoyed a pleasant spin along the Ring Road before pulling into Cotton Town exactly on schedule. This was fortunate because Hoskins was standing just inside the gate timing everyone in. He gave me a little sort of friendly nod as we passed by, but I paid him no attention at all and went straight across the yard before reversing back onto the loading bay. We were supposed to spend the next fifteen minutes waiting by the vehicle on the off-chance that someone would come and unload it before one o'clock. In reality, of course, the morning was already considered to be over, so after a quick check to make sure Hoskins was still busily engaged at the gateway, we slipped off for dinner.

'Coming up the canteen?' asked George. 'Game of cards?'

'No,' I said. 'I'll go over to the cafe I think.'

'OK, see you later.'

'Yeah, see you.'

At half past one I was back on the bay giving the van's windscreen a polish. Then I slid open the roller door and looked inside. It was hardly what you would call a full load. Nearest me, about halfway back, was a single pallet stacked with medium crates. Beyond this, a number of empty pallets were piled up next to a pallet full of empty crates. With the aid of a trolley I could have unloaded the whole lot, on my own, in about ten minutes. But this wasn't the way of things on The Scheme, so instead I sat on the concrete edge and waited. Actually, I quite liked being here at this time of day when all was quiet. There was no sign of Hoskins, and as far as I could see Watts's office was deserted. My only company was the half-dozen UniVans that stood lined along the bay, waiting for their afternoon duties to begin. Beyond them the emergency fire hose lay coiled around its drum. I enjoyed the silent hiatus for a further ten minutes, and then at last heard feet returning.

'I saw Steve Armstrong up in the darts room,' George announced. 'Playing on his own.'

'Was he winning?' I enquired.

'Dunno, but he was being a bit funny, I thought.'

'Why?'

'Well, I asked him how come he wasn't out with Steve Moore today, and he just sort of looked at the dartboard and said, "I've been stood down." You know, all abrupt like.'

'Didn't he give a reason?'

'No, he didn't, and then Jumo Williams came in and they started practising, so I came out.'

'I expect there's a simple explanation.'

'I hope so,' said George. 'I don't like it when people are being funny.'

2

The honour of unloading our vehicle eventually fell to
Kevin Jennings. He came from nowhere riding a forklift
truck, at exactly the same time as Watts appeared on
the stairway. Both were fifteen minutes late, but they
were punctual in relation to one another. Watts entered
his office and closed the door without engaging the
latch, so that it slowly swung open again by about six
inches.

Kevin made a direct line for us.

'Now then, what have we got here?' he said, entering
the van and sliding his forks under the laden pallet.

'Twenty-four mediums,' I replied.

'That's what it says on my sheet.' He raised the load
and brought it out into the daylight. 'Four sixes are
twenty-four. Yep, that's right.'

'Hold it a minute!' Watts had suddenly come out of

his office and was advancing upon us. 'Let me have a quick look at those labels.'

Kevin, George and I watched as he walked around the stack of crates, squinting at each one in turn. Then he peered at me. 'What are these?'

'Should be rear offside winker attachments.'

'Should be,' he said. 'But aren't. According to the labels they're all rear nearside.'

'Doesn't make any difference, does it?'

'Course it does. They wink differently. Who loaded you?'

'Er . . . well, what does it say on the docket?'

'Name's indecipherable. As usual.'

'Oh, right,' I said, gazing at George. 'Let's see. Er . . . Martin, wasn't it?'

'No,' said George. 'It was Chris, I think.'

'Or it could have been the other Chris.'

'Yes, it possibly could. Or maybe . . .'

'Alright, alright!' interrupted Watts. 'It's not a hanging offence. No one's going to get hanged. But this is the second time in a fortnight we've had the wrong crates come in from Long Reach. Last week it was front nearside winker attachments.'

'Do they wink differently as well?' I asked.

'No,' he said, giving me an unblinking stare. 'Fortunately, they don't.'

It was hard to tell just how seriously Watts took his work, but he didn't question me further, nor me him. At that moment the external telephone bells began ringing. 'Righto,' he said, casting a glance at Kevin.

'Mark 'em up and park 'em up. I think I'll have to have a word with that lot and wake their ideas up a little bit.'

'What's he talking about them winking differently?' said George, as soon as Watts was back in his office.

'Oh, take no notice of him,' replied Kevin. 'He hasn't got anything better to do, that's all.'

From his pocket he produced a piece of yellow wax crayon and marked each crate with the letters LR. Also the day's date. Then he boarded his forklift and ferried the load into the depths of the storage area. He came back a short time later with a full-size crate.

'This for Blackwell?' I asked.

'Yep,' he said. 'Roller Guides. Four Dozen.'

'Ah, that's what I love about this job,' remarked George. 'The variety.'

'Anything for Merry Park?'

'Not today,' replied Kevin.

'That's handy.'

I spoke too soon, because next thing I noticed Watts emerging once again from his hideaway.

'Just a minute,' he said, walking up. 'Looks like we might have something else for you as well. I've just had a phone call from Bob Little at Long Reach. Merry Park have been onto him for a pallet trolley. There's nothing available at his end, so he wanted to know if we could spare one from here.'

'I hope you told him no.'

'As a matter of fact, I didn't,' replied Watts. 'We've got an idle one out the back, haven't we Kevin?'

'Yep,' came the answer. 'Hasn't been used for a while though.'

'That's alright,' said Watts. 'Probably only needs a drop of grease. Pop and get it can you?'

'OK.'

As Kevin wandered towards the gloomy rear of the building I turned to Watts and said, 'Does that mean we've got to go to Merry Park?'

'Course you've got to go to Merry Park,' he announced, producing the schedules book from his pocket and finding the relevant page. 'Yes, it's your last call.'

'But we were hoping to miss it out today,' I said.

'Miss it out?'

'Cos there's been nothing to go there all week.'

'And nothing to pick up,' added George. 'We've been running the last leg empty.'

Out of the corner of my eye I saw a movement, and in the same instant realized that Hoskins had joined us. He'd been out in the yard all morning, and was wearing his complete outfit, including black coat and black peaked cap. Watts, meanwhile, was clad in the standard indoor black jacket. Mutually reinforced, the two officials looked at me with apparent disbelief.

'How long you been on The Scheme?' Watts asked.

'About five years,' I replied.

'Well then,' he said. 'You should know very well you can't go missing out ports of call just because it takes your fancy.'

'But I thought someone might sign the card for us, as it's quiet.'

'Who do you mean by "someone"?'

'Dunno really.'

'Mr Gosling, for example?'

'No, of course not.'

'Well, who then?'

'It depends.'

A long silence followed, during which Watts stood slowly shaking his head as if reminded of some unbearable tragedy of long ago. Meanwhile, Hoskins took a half-turn away, for no apparent reason other than to gaze across the yard with a mournful expression on his face.

'Look,' said Watts at last. 'They need a spare trolley at Merry Park and you're the only van going from here to there. If you're looking for an early swerve you can forget about it.'

'Alright,' I answered, with a shrug. 'It was worth a try though, wasn't it?'

'Not in our book,' said Hoskins, finally breaking his authoritative silence. 'Definitely not in our book.'

Without a further word, the pair walked slowly and deliberately back to their den. Hoskins went inside first, followed by Watts, who gave us a last significant look before closing the door.

'They think they're so superior sometimes, don't they?' murmured George.

'Yeah,' I agreed.

'It's different when they want a favour doing, of course.'

These last words were drowned out by a dreadful squealing noise from deep within the building. It was Kevin returning with the spare pallet trolley.

'They're going to have some fun with this up the Park,' he said. 'I don't think it's been used for about a year.'

'What do they need a trolley for anyway?' I asked. 'They've got plenty of forklifts there.'

'Emergency back-up,' explained Kevin. 'There's a memo been round saying there has to be at least one manual trolley on hand at each depot, just in case.'

'In case of what?'

'It didn't say.'

'Alright,' I said. 'I suppose if we've got to take it we've got to take it. Do you want me to sign for this one?'

'You'd better, yes. Otherwise it won't have gone anywhere, officially.'

So I signed Kevin's docket, then we got the trolley into the van, secured it to the bulkhead, and closed the roller door. In another minute George and I were pulling out of Cotton Town, the two of us feeling quite irritated. Watts's interference had effectively transformed a pleasant afternoon's cruise into a race against time, and what made it worse was that it could have been so easily avoided. There was obviously no pressing demand for a spare trolley up at Merry Park. All Watts needed to have done when Bob Little rang was fob him off until the following day, or maybe even the following week. Instead, he had to go and insist that we take one up there straightaway, which meant that all our careful plans were laid to waste. We'd been pacing ourselves nicely since dinner time, not getting loaded too quickly and having a bit of a chat with Kevin. Then we were going to have a gentle meander over to Blackwell, arriving just in time for a cup of tea. This unforeseen delay over the pallet trolley now meant that we were going to have to rush about all afternoon just to keep on schedule!

'Typical!' I said, as we sped out past the gatehouse and onto the road. 'Flaming typical!'

'Don't forget I've still got to have a word with Osgood,' said George.

'Well, you'll have to be quick about it. We can't hang about there for long if we want to finish on time.'

I sensed that he was about to raise a voice in protest, but instead he fell silent and sat gazing at the lone cake box, still sitting on top of the dashboard.

And so it was that we began our return run back towards Blackwell depot. I hated being late, unless it was pre-planned, of course, and so I gunned that poor UniVan through half a dozen sets of amber lights and onto the Ring Road. From here it was due west in a stream of traffic that fortunately turned out to be quite light. By the time we passed Sandro's Bakery, now closed up for the day, we were more or less back on schedule, although I was still having to shove along at a fair old rate.

'They've got no power, these things!' I complained, shouting above the tortured engine. 'Second gear's too low and third's too high!'

'And they're too noisy!' said George.

'Pardon?'

I was feeling in a slightly better mood when we finally arrived at Blackwell, pausing at the end of the yard for George to jump out with his cake. Over on the bay I could see Len talking to Bill Harper. They looked like they'd just finished loading Bill's van. As I reversed in next to it I noticed a stranger sitting in the dummy seat, busily writing something down. He glanced at me momentarily when I got out and walked round to the steps, then he continued writing. I joined Bill on the bay, Len having disappeared for the time being.

'Hello, mate,' I said. 'Who's that in your cab?'

'It's a new bloke learning the run,' Bill replied. 'Doing it by the book, he is, noting down all the turnings and depot names. I keep telling him he'll know it off by heart after a week or two, but he won't listen.'

'Might as well let him get on with it then.'

'Yeah.'

'Where's he going to be based?'

'Long Reach.'

'Oh, lucky him.'

'Lucky all of us.'

'Yes,' I agreed. 'Lucky all of us.'

Bill smiled and glanced towards the office. 'Right, I'd better get moving. Osgood's peeping out. Is that George in there with him?'

'Yeah, he's gone to ask a favour.'

'Cakes?'

'You guessed it.'

After Bill had gone I opened the roller door and looked in at the single crate I'd brought from Cotton Town. It then occurred to me that Len must have forgotten I had something for him. I was just about to go upstairs and seek him out when Gosling came sauntering along the bay.

'Something the matter?' he asked.

'Well,' I replied. 'I could do with getting going fairly smartish, but there's no sign of Len.'

'That's unlike him,' Gosling remarked. 'He's usually very scrupulous about unloading people straightaway. What have you got for us?'

'Just one full-sizer.'

'Tell you what then,' he said. 'I'll unload you myself. I could do with a little bit of practice.'

There was a forklift truck standing a few yards away, and the moment Gosling boarded it and started up I understood exactly what he meant. Obviously he hadn't operated such equipment for a long time, no doubt due to Len's strict monopoly of the loading bay. I quickly stepped clear as the truck lurched towards me and then stopped again.

'Bit light on the throttle,' announced Gosling as he moved forward once more. This time he seemed to have gained a degree of control. I watched as he manoeuvred carefully behind our UniVan, and drove the forklift inside. Then its motor fell silent. A few seconds later Gosling emerged on foot.

'What's up?' I asked.

'Battery's flat,' he replied.

'Stuck is it?'

'Well and truly.'

'What are you doing?!' roared a voice from the back of the bay. It was Len returning on board another forklift. His face was like thunder as he sped up and stopped beside us. 'What are you doing?!'

'I was just getting this van unloaded,' said Gosling. 'Since you seemed to have disappeared.'

'Don't give me that!' snapped Len. 'I've been to get the other truck! That one in there's got a dodgy battery!'

'Yes, I've just found out.'

'Didn't you notice the warning light was on?!'

'No, I didn't. Sorry.'

This exchange was interesting to observe because Gosling was supposed to be in charge of Len, not the other way round. Here was a superintendent apologizing for his actions while a mere warehouseman sat on top of a forklift truck and shouted at him. It would have been quite unheard of at some depots. In one sense I felt sorry for Gosling because he had meant well. At the same time I firmly believed that supers should never meddle with the smooth running of things. Already this afternoon I'd had to put up with Watts's intervention over the pallet trolley, and now there was this episode. Len clearly had everything under control before Gosling came along and put a spanner in the works. The result was that I was going to be stuck at Blackwell for another half-hour while the problem was sorted out. A stalled forklift truck couldn't be moved when the power failed, so with a look of disgust on his face Len marched over to the workshops in search of a mechanic. George, meanwhile, had returned from his dealings with Osgood. He took one look at the situation and understood it in an instant.

'Back in a minute,' he said, heading towards the canteen stairs.

While these minor events were unfolding, I'd noticed Gosling glance once or twice in the direction of the office. This made me wonder whether he was seeking support from Osgood, or simply hoping that his humiliation hadn't been witnessed by a fellow super. For humiliation it most certainly was. When Len finally came back with the mechanic, Bob Smith, they both practically ignored Gosling. He stood and watched awkwardly as Bob removed the engine cover and examined the battery. Then the verdict was given.

'Drained beyond recovery,' Bob announced. 'I'll have to put a new one in.'

This meant a visit to the stores. Gosling signed the necessary requisition docket, and then Bob wandered away, slowly shaking his head and asking if people thought he had nothing better to do than run around repairing forklifts.

The stairwell door swung open, and George came through it backwards with a tray bearing five cups.

'Tea up!' he called. 'There's one for you as well, Bob! I'll leave it by the steps!'

Now I had to admit George was very good at this kind of thing. He possessed a fine grasp of human sensitivities, and the way he went about presenting the cups of tea was a lesson in diplomacy. First of all he approached Len, who accepted his with quiet grace, having been told there were two sugars in it, of course. Then George put the other drinks aside before going over to Gosling, who was gazing along the bay with a forlorn expression on his face.

'Here you are, Mr Gosling. Thought you might like one too.'

It wasn't the usual practice to buy teas for superintendents, and Gosling certainly wouldn't have been expecting such a gesture. Therefore he showed both surprise and gratitude when the cup was offered to him.

'Thank you, George,' he said. 'That's most kind.'

3

As the minutes passed there was a chance that Osgood would suddenly decide to leave his office and come to find out what was causing the delay. Technically he and Gosling were of equal rank, since both wore silver badges, but there was no doubt that Osgood was higher in the pecking order. If he had turned up at that moment then subsequent events might have taken a completely different course. As it was, he must have decided that Gosling was quite capable of sorting out whatever problem there may be, and so remained at his desk.

By now a couple more UniVans had turned up in the yard, and their drivers were standing around waiting to be unloaded. Gosling looked quite relieved when Len went off to deal with them. Bob Smith, meanwhile, had come back and set about fixing the forklift. I thought he made quite a fuss about putting the new battery in, considering he was an engineer who could take a UniVan to pieces in a day. He puffed and blowed and fiddled around getting it connected, and made it clear he'd much rather be over in the workshops doing a 'proper' repair job than wasting his valuable time with us. Finally, however, he was done.

'That's it,' he said, turning to Gosling. 'Try to be a bit more careful in future.'

After Bob had gone I took the forklift and unloaded the UniVan myself, even though Gosling was standing right there on the bay beside us. Drivers weren't supposed to operate forklift trucks, but I knew he wouldn't say anything, and he didn't. Not with that nice hot cup of tea inside him.

'I take it there's nothing to go to Merry Park?' I queried. 'There hasn't been all week.'

'Er . . . no, no,' replied Gosling after a glance at his worksheet. 'No, Len would have said if there was, wouldn't he?'

'Usually does, yes.'

'Right, well, you might as well get moving then.'

'Have you seen the time?' asked George.

Gosling peered at his watch. 'Dear oh dear,' he said. 'I hadn't noticed. You'll never make it to Merry Park by four o'clock. Where's that pallet trolley supposed to be going?'

'Up the Park.'

'Well, it can't be urgent,' Gosling announced. 'Tell you what. Give me your duty card, and I'll sign you straight back to Long Reach. Otherwise you'll be finishing after your scheduled time.'

I'd never seen George move so quick. He was down the steps, into the cab, and back with the card in about thirty seconds. Next thing Gosling was writing his badge number and signature, next to the words WORKING TO INSTRUCTION.

Which meant we'd got our early swerve after all.

With no more deliveries to make that day, all we had to do was take the UniVan back to Long Reach depot. Then we could go home.

'Don't make it too obvious,' I murmured to George, as we headed down the loading-bay steps. 'You know how Len feels about people getting signed off before their proper time.'

Fortunately, Len was busily engaged when we pulled out of the yard, and probably didn't even see us go. It'd come to that hour of the working day when The Scheme cranked itself back into life. Blackwell had seemed quite deserted when we'd arrived in mid-afternoon, but now preparations were being made for the return of the UniVans. Just before we left, Mick Dalston and Charlie Green had materialized from somewhere inside the building, no doubt to give Len a hand, while Osgood got ready to stir from his office. In other parts of the depot, clerks, managers and canteen ladies would be watching the clock slowly tick round, as would engineers, keymasters, gatemen and janitorial staff. Even as we departed, vans were beginning to trickle through the gates in a desultory manner, and by the time we'd got onto the Ring Road there seemed to be UniVans everywhere, all heading back to their respective depots. This flurry of activity happened daily as the vehicles made their final runs home. Some might have been parked for the last hour in a discreet but convenient lay-by, waiting for the correct moment. Others may have strayed off-route on missions of their own. The majority, however, would simply have been carrying out their legitimate duties, pursuing schedules which brought them back to their home base at twenty past four, or thereabouts. That was the intention anyway. In reality, vans began to appear at the gates any time from four onwards, even though their crews wouldn't be allowed to clock off for another half-hour.

They also risked being booked by the supers, who frowned on people who returned too early. When we pulled into Long Reach there were already a number of vans gathered in the yard, and Collis was marching around generally berating their drivers.

'Look, lads,' he was saying. 'We don't mind you taking your ten-off-the-eight for locking up. We don't mind that at all, it was agreed years ago, but you're pushing it a bit at five past four, aren't you? Try and do your flat day, can you, lads? It's only eight hours after all.'

No one took the slightest bit of notice of him.

The only person with a passable excuse was Bill Harper, who'd managed to get his UniVan into the vehicle wash before anyone else, just as he did every other day of the week. He now stood watching while the great rollers turned, and gallons of water gushed over the gleaming paintwork. The supers were unlikely to challenge a man who kept his van so clean.

When I showed Collis our signed duty card he directed me to pull straight onto the loading bay. Gosling's signature meant we didn't have to wait to clock off today, so I turned to George and said, 'Off you go then, have a good holiday and don't worry about your cakes.'

'Thanks,' he replied, climbing out. 'See you two weeks Monday.'

'Yeah, bye.'

There was one other UniVan parked on the bay. I glanced at its running plates and recognized it as the vehicle I'd seen Steve Moore driving that morning when we'd crossed paths on the Ring Road. Then I saw Steve himself, ascending the stairway towards the main offices.

'Steve!' I called.

I was sure that he'd heard me, but instead of responding he merely quickened his pace and carried on up the stairs. By the time I'd got out of the van he'd gone. He obviously wasn't inclined to talk, so I locked up, handed in the keys and headed home.

That was Friday. The following Monday I clocked on at ten to eight, and then went into the duty room to see Bob Little. He was behind the counter as usual, poring over his schedules chart as if it held the secret to some eternal puzzle.

'Morning, Bob,' I said. 'Who've you got for me this week?'

'Ah, morning,' he said, glancing up. 'Actually, we'd like you to take a new recruit if you don't mind.'

'A new recruit?' I repeated. 'What about Dave Parfitt or Pete Fentiman? Can't I have one of them?'

'Sorry,' Bob answered. 'They're already spoken for.'

'Who've I got then?'

'Assistant Driver Jonathan Fairley. He needs someone to show him the ropes. We thought you'd be best.'

The way Bob said 'we' made it sound as if some standing committee had specially requested that I look after the newcomer, and that his future on The Scheme would be dependent on the invaluable advice only I could give him. The truth, of course, was much more simple: no one else was available.

'Yeah, alright,' I said. 'But I'll expect a favour in return.'

'Naturally,' Bob replied. 'Oh, by the way, did anyone mention to you about a pallet trolley for Merry Park?'

'Er . . . yes. There was a spare one over at Blackwell. We picked it up Friday.'

'That's good,' said Bob. 'Maybe they'll stop pestering me about it now.'

'Where is this Jonathan person then?'

'I sent him to look for you. Expect he's out there somewhere. Be nice to him, won't you?'

'Course I will. See you later.'

'Bye.'

I found Jonathan out in the corridor. He was examining the duty rota, and the moment I laid eyes on him I knew he was new. At this time of day there were lots of people milling around as everybody clocked on and got their vans ready for the day's run. Most of them were known to me, either by name or at least to say hello to, and what they all had in common were their uniforms, which without exception lacked crispness. This new recruit, on the other hand, looked like a tailor's dummy. His shirt, trousers and jacket were obviously fresh from their wrappers that very morning, and held him in a stiff pose as he stood looking at the rota. Once they'd been through a washing machine or dry cleaner's they'd look like a normal set of clothes, but for the moment he appeared quite uncomfortable.

'That rota won't make any sense until you've been here a while,' I said, by way of greeting.

'Well, I was just trying to make head or tail of it really,' Jonathan replied. 'I've already had several looks at it.'

'Not to worry: you'll soon pick it up. How long have you been on The Scheme?'

'Ten days.'

'So you'll have done your basic training?'

'Yes.'

'Tell you what then: I'll get us a cup of tea and a doughnut apiece, while you collect the keys for the van. Do you know where the key room is?'

'Yep.'

'Right, it's UV55. I'll meet you on the bay.'

He marched off in the wrong direction before realizing his mistake and turning back. Meanwhile, I went across the road to the cafe, where tea was served three or possibly four times faster than upstairs in the canteen. Then I walked round to the loading bay and waited. A dozen or more UniVans were backed in, all with their engines running so that their cab heaters could warm up. Mine was parked next to Bill Harper's, and he was standing at the rear watching Chris Peachment get him loaded. Along the entire length of the bay there was similar activity, as fully-laden pallets were moved around by men on forklift trucks. In the meantime, Horsefall was observing the scene from his office at the far end. The fact that he remained ensconced indicated operations were running smoothly that morning.

When Bill saw me he came over for a chat.

'Richard back from his holidays yet?' I asked.

'No,' Bill replied. 'He's got another week left.'

'How come you don't go away together then?'

'It doesn't work out like that does it? Just because we're brothers. Even if we were a married couple they'd probably give us our holidays separate.'

'Suppose.'

'Besides,' he added. 'I spend enough time with him all week. I don't want to go on holiday with him as well.'

'Who've you got this week then?'

'Same as last week. You know, that bloke learning the run.'

'Oh yeah,' I said. 'I've got a new recruit too.'

'What's he like?'

'Seems OK. How about yours?'

'Not sure,' said Bill. 'Remember I told you he was writing down all the details?'

'Yeah.'

'Well, he keeps asking questions all the time. Driving me up the wall. Wants to know why we go from this depot to that, and why we have to leave at certain times and so on.'

'Can't you tell him that's just how it is?'

'I do,' said Bill. 'But he wants to know why.'

Just then Jonathan came back with a worried look on his face.

'Get the keys alright?' I asked.

'Er . . . no, I didn't,' he replied. 'That man behind the hatch wouldn't give me them.'

When he heard this Bill smiled and shook his head.

'Oh, yes, sorry,' I said. 'I should have warned you. You've got to be careful how you deal with Arthur. What did you say to him, exactly?'

'Just, "Can I have the keys for UV55?"'

'Is that all?'

'Yes. Well . . . no.'

'What, then?'

'The thing is, when I got there he was round the corner out of sight, so I had to stick my head through the hatch to get his attention. I think my actual words were, "Excuse me, can I have the keys for UV55?"'

'And what did he say?'

'"No, you can't."'

'He's getting worse and worse,' remarked Bill.

'Right, look,' I explained. 'Arthur's quite touchy about who he gives the keys to, and if you get on the wrong side of him he can be very awkward.'

'What did I say wrong then?' asked Jonathan.

'Nothing probably, but he might have thought you were being sarcastic.'

'So how do I get the keys?'

'Tell you what,' I said. 'Horsefall's peeping out. I'll get them today or we'll be late leaving. Here you are. Have a cup of tea and a doughnut.'

'Thanks,' said Jonathan. 'How much do I owe you?'

'Nothing. You don't have to pay on your first day.'

I left Bill explaining the best way to approach Arthur, and went off to see if I could fare any more successfully. When I got to the key room the hatch was closed, which was always a bad sign, but after a couple of polite knocks Arthur opened it. Behind him was an array of keys, all hanging on numbered hooks.

'Yes?'

'Morning, Arthur,' I said. 'Fifty-five please.'

'Fifty-five?'

'Yes, please.'

'Seems to be very popular all of a sudden,' he said, turning to the key rack and reaching for the appropriate bunch. 'I've just had someone else come along asking for these.'

'Yes,' I said. 'I sent him.'

'Oh, you sent him, did you?' said Arthur. 'Must be nice having someone running round at your beck and call. Very nice indeed.'

He continued holding the keys, allowing them to dangle from his index finger as he stood regarding me through the hatch. I glanced at the clock above him. It was ten past eight.

'To tell you the truth,' I said. 'I'm in a bit of a hurry.'

'Yes,' replied Arthur. 'Your friend was in a bit of a hurry too. Everyone's in a bit of a hurry. Everyone expects me to jump.'

Slowly and deliberately he turned to a ledger on the desk beside him, took a pencil and added the figure 55 to a long list. Then, at last, he handed me the keys.

'Thanks,' I said.

'That's alright,' said Arthur, closing the hatch.

When I got back to the bay Chris Peachment was waiting with a forklift truck and several pallets. He was talking to Jonathan and they seemed to be getting on alright. By now most of the other vans had departed, but there were still a few being loaded, here and there. I unlocked the roller door and looked in at the pallet trolley from Friday, still waiting to be delivered to Merry Park. Then Chris got the stuff inside, and a few minutes later we were ready to leave.

'Right,' I said to Jonathan. 'Do you know where we're going?'

'Yes,' he replied. 'I looked it up in the duty room. We go from here to Blackwell depot, then Cotton Town. Dinner there, then we go back to Blackwell, then Merry Park and back here.'

'Very good.'

'How come we go to Blackwell twice?'

'It's just the way the schedules are worked out,' I explained. 'Don't forget we have to marry up with other vans from other depots. It's so that we keep everything moving round all the time.'

'But doesn't it get boring, going back to the same place?'

'That's nothing,' I said. 'Some duties are much more repetitive. Take number sixteen, for example. That's here to Rudgeway and back, four times.'

'Blimey.' Jonathan looked quite dismayed at the prospect.

'Don't worry,' I said. 'All the journeys have been properly timed and so forth. It's a doddle actually.'

'And when will I get to do some driving?'

'Ooh, not for a long time yet. You've got to sit it out as an assistant first, and learn your relevant runs. But you'll get behind the wheel eventually.'

'When though?'

'Couple of years.'

'Oh.'

'Look, it's twenty past eight, we'd better get moving. Did you get the docket off Chris?'

'Yep.'

'Right, let's go.'

When I went round to the front of the van I discovered a note wedged under the windscreen wipers. It said: PLEASE CALL AT WORKSHOP RE CAKES.

'Ah, yes,' I said, out loud. 'I'd forgotten all about them.'

'Forgotten what?' said Jonathan.

'Nothing of importance,' I replied. 'Jump in.'

Instead of heading for the main gates I drove the van in a long arc across the yard, stopping next to the engineer's shop. Then I got out and fiddled around with the offside mirror, as if checking it was adjusted properly.

A voice behind me said, 'I've got something for you.'

Rob Marshall was standing in the workshop doorway with a big grin on his face.

'Oh,' I said, 'George roped you in too did he? I wondered how he was going to fix things at this end.'

Rob led me to a bench inside. It was stacked up with about twelve pink and white boxes.

'What's this?' I said. 'He told me it was only going to be a few.'

'That's what he said to me as well,' Rob replied. 'Then this lot turned up at half past seven this morning.'

'Who brought them in?'

'Don't know. They just suddenly appeared while we were all busy out the back.'

'I'll wring his neck.'

Rob helped me get the boxes into the cab on Jonathan's side, which was obscured from prying eyes. I had no doubt that Horsefall knew all about George's cakes and had been suitably squared. Even so, it would do no harm to keep the whole operation low-key, just in case. Jonathan looked as if he was about to say something when we piled the boxes around him, but then changed his mind. Instead, he sat in the dummy seat looking rather uneasy.

When we finally left Long Reach there was only one other vehicle in the yard. A lone UniVan remained parked on the bay, and when we went past I saw the driver sitting in the cab. It was Steve Moore, all on his own again. This time I didn't bother to wave. We rolled out through the gates and headed for the Ring Road, on Jonathan's first day as an assistant driver.

The picture for duty number seventeen was the usual one. Everything we'd picked up that morning, the entire load, was bound for Blackwell. After that I had no idea what we would be collecting or taking onward to the other depots, and this unknown quantity helped reduce the monotony of the job. Jonathan, however, wanted to know all the details, and kept up a barrage of questions for the entire journey. I was reminded of Bill Harper's words when he told me how his trainee was driving him up the wall. Now, apparently, it was my turn.

On the other hand, it was good that these newcomers were keen to learn about The Scheme and all its inner workings, and I suspected that the enquiries would subside after a while.

We pulled into Blackwell dead on schedule, despite our late start. Several other vans were already being dealt with, but there was a space on the bay so I reversed into it. Within minutes Len Walker had appeared with his forklift and begun unloading. Meanwhile, Jonathan wandered amongst the various stacks of crates, pausing from time to time to study their labels.

'Where's Eden Lacy?' he asked at length.

'Don't know,' I replied. 'It must be one of the depots outside our radius. Don't forget there are hundreds of them scattered all over the place. It could be anywhere in the country. What else does it say?'

'Size 2 rubber grommets: one gross. Stocks Green, Long Reach, Blackwell, Eden Lacy.'

'Right,' I said. 'Every picture tells a story. Some time or other that crate will be collected from here and taken to Eden Lacy depot. Maybe they're short of grommets up there. Or maybe not. They might just move them on again after a while.'

While we'd been talking Len had finished his unloading and was now standing nearby, listening with interest. After the mid-morning burst of activity Blackwell had begun to wind down towards dinner. Further along the bay Charlie Green was occupied with the only other remaining van. Except that occupied wasn't really the right word. In the time Len had taken to empty us, Charlie had managed to remove one pallet from his vehicle, having spent most of the intervening minutes talking to the driver. By rights, Gosling or Osgood or one of the other superintendents should have come along and told him to get a move on, but for the moment there was no sign of any of them, so Charlie just continued his conversation. Len shook his head with obvious disdain, then headed upstairs to the games room. Jonathan and I made ready to depart.

When we got back in the cab I saw the stack of cake boxes and remembered I had to call in at Sandro's.

There was plenty of time, so when I did the drop I made sure not to involve Jonathan, carrying the cakes into the bakery in two lots by myself. Sandro was up to his ears in work, as were his three colleagues, but we exchanged pleasantries nonetheless.

'How are you, my friend?' he asked, taking a great armful of boxes from me.

'Fine, thanks,' I replied. 'You look busy.'

'Oh, busy, busy, busy!' he said. 'Always busy!'

I looked at the beads of sweat rolling down his forehead, and wondered how long Charlie Green would last in such a place.

As usual, there was one box to collect, the one that had to be transferred to Pete Giggs on run number seven. When I returned with it to the UniVan, Jonathan at last broke his silence concerning the boxes.

'Don't mind my asking,' he said. 'But isn't it prohibited to carry goods in the cab?'

'It isn't a good,' I replied. 'It's a cake.'

'But all the same . . .'

'Look,' I said. 'Don't worry about it. No one's going to ask questions about one box, and even if they do I'll take full responsibility, OK?'

'Well, as long as you're sure.'

'Course I am. The management aren't bothered about that sort of thing. Their only concern is to keep these vans on schedule, so all the collections and deliveries coincide. That's all they're interested in, so just relax and enjoy the ride, same as everyone else does.'

'Alright,' said Jonathan. 'I'll try my best.'

'And don't forget you're being paid for the pleasure.'

This last remark put a smile on his face, and as he settled back in the dummy seat I sensed he was beginning to feel more at ease. Soon we had resumed our noonward journey to Cotton Town, cruising along the Ring Road with plenty of time to ponder the advantages of life on The Scheme. After all, what could be nicer than an excursion in a UniVan on a bright spring morning? Oh, I admit they were under-powered and rattly, and that the novelty of driving them wore off once you'd done a few years behind the wheel. But every so often, when I caught sight of my vehicle reflected in some huge glass-fronted office building, it seemed there could be no better way to earn a living.

For without a doubt the UniVan was a glorious creation! With its distinctive gunmetal paintwork and silver livery, its bull-nosed profile, running boards and chrome front grill, it had become a celebrated national icon, recognized and loved by all! Moreover, it represented a great idea that not only worked, but was seen to work!

Having said that, there were some people whose passion for UniVans seemed to go a bit too far. As we came onto an elevated section of road I noticed a group of men with notebooks sitting on a concrete buttress. When we passed by they all peered at us intently.

'Who are they?' asked Jonathan, when I pointed them out to him.

'Enthusiasts,' I replied. 'They like writing down the numbers.'

'But I thought that was just for children.'

'Ooh no,' I said. 'That lot take it all very seriously. They know the schedules better than the supers do, and some of them even own their own vans.'

'Where do they get them from?'

'They're auctioned off after a hundred thousand miles.'

'And they go out in them, do they?'

'No, they don't. They would if they could, but it's not allowed, so they keep them in their gardens.'

'Well, why don't they just get jobs on The Scheme?' Jonathan suggested. 'Then they could ride round to their heart's content.'

'Don't ask me,' I replied. 'They're barmy, that lot.'

Oddly enough, having seemingly convinced Jonathan that being paid to drive a UniVan was quite an enviable existence, I now began to have a troubling thought of my own. It was hardly anything really, nothing more than a vague irritation, but it was there alright. As far as I could tell it had been triggered off at Blackwell when we'd come across the label that said Eden Lacy. At first, I couldn't think why the name of some remote and unknown depot should bother me so much. Then I realized it was precisely because I'd never been there. Despite having done five years on The Scheme, covering many miles of road, I'd only actually visited the seven depots on our circuit, namely, Blackwell, Cotton Town, Rudgeway, Bell Tower, Stocks Green, Merry Park and, of course, Long Reach. I also knew the locations of Royal Pond and Castle Gate depots, though I'd never had occasion to go to either of them. Eden Lacy, however, was a name I hadn't heard before, and it struck me that as much as I enjoyed my job, there was something restrictive about always travelling along the same few routes, back and forth, week in, week out. Wouldn't it be nice, I thought, just for once to go to a different destination.

As if on cue I noticed a grey flash somewhere down to my right. We were still on the elevated section, with fine views over a vast expanse of rooftops, parks and gardens. Below us was the former arterial highway, which had been superseded a decade earlier when the Ring Road was built. Nowadays, freed from the burden of heavy traffic, it had become a pleasant, spacious avenue. And rolling along it was a lone UniVan, bound for who-knows-where.

4

When we returned to Blackwell that afternoon the first thing I had to do was go and see Osgood. Leaving Jonathan in charge of our UniVan, I took the single cake box and headed for the office. Osgood was there, looking very relaxed with his feet up on the desk.

'Don't tell me,' he said, when he caught sight of the box. 'One cake to be transferred to Pete Giggs.'

'Yes, please,' I replied. 'If you don't mind.'

'George got you running round for him, has he?'

'Yeah, I had to shift about a dozen this morning.'

'I didn't quite catch that,' said Osgood. 'And you'd better hide that one underneath here. I've heard Nesbitt's on the prowl.'

'Nesbitt?' I said, dismayed. 'What's he doing in these parts?'

'You tell me. No one knows how his mind works.

Sometimes we don't see him for months on end, then suddenly he decides to pay a visit. Apparently he turned up at the Bell Tower the other day without any warning. Sat in the super's room for eight hours. Never uttered a word.'

'Well, I hope he doesn't come here.'

'So do I,' said Osgood. 'Believe me, so do I.'

I put the cake under his desk, thanked him and then returned to the bay, where Len and Jonathan were now deep in conversation.

'I hope you're setting him a good example,' said Len, as I joined them. 'Keeping him on the straight and narrow.'

'Doing my best,' I replied.

'That's good. We don't want him drifting into the other sphere of influence.'

One look at Jonathan told me he had no idea what Len was talking about. However, I didn't bother trying to explain it all to him, as I knew it wouldn't be long until he found out for himself. At the same time, I realized that Len had come to regard me as an ally in the crusade he'd embarked upon, namely, to conserve the eight-hour 'flat' day.

Now I have to say I could see Len's point. The success of The Scheme depended above all else on appearances. It was popular because people could see it in operation on a daily basis. When a UniVan passed by, it reminded onlookers that all across the country men and women were occupied in gainful employment. Eight hours' work for eight hours' pay: that was the deal, and everyone agreed it was fair. What worried Len was the number of early finishes that were being dished out by lenient superintendents. He saw this as a threat to The Scheme's public support, and he obviously thought I agreed with him. Well, of course I did in principle, but to tell the truth I quite liked the occasional early swerve, as we called it. It was a nice treat to go home at four o'clock on the odd day if things were quiet. Or half past three even. Certainly, it wasn't a perk I took for granted, but neither did I wish to give it up entirely. As for Len's reference to 'the other sphere of influence', he presumably meant Charlie Green and his ilk. True, Charlie did push it occasionally, especially when soft touches like Gosling were near at hand. All in all, though, I remained convinced that Len's fears were groundless.

One thing I knew for sure was that Jonathan and I would be getting no early swerve today. We still had that pallet trolley from Friday on board the van, waiting to go to Merry Park, so there was no avoiding the final journey. Len unloaded three pallets that we'd brought over from Cotton Town, then I closed the roller door and flipped the catch. As we departed I noticed him give Jonathan a friendly pat on the back.

'Very important place, Merry Park,' I said, as we pulled out of the front gates. 'It's the central hub for this region. Any amount of UniVans pass through there, from all over the place.'

'So how come we've got nothing to deliver except the trolley?' asked Jonathan.

'Good question,' I replied. 'Yes, it has been a bit quiet

lately, but that doesn't mean a thing. Sometimes you can be packed to the gunwales all day long: it just depends what comes in from the different depots. When it's like this we just try to make the most of it.'

'So we don't just run round empty all the time?'

'Oh, no. Quite the opposite.'

As a matter of fact, Jonathan's observation wasn't as far off the mark as I'd made out. When I thought about it, I hadn't actually been to Merry Park since the Tuesday of the previous week, and as far as I could remember that was just to deliver a single full-size crate. Prior to that, I had no recollection of taking more than the odd pallet there for several months, or possibly even longer. It then dawned on me that despite Merry Park's reputation as being a pivotal component in the smooth running of The Scheme, the truth was that its daily workload was only light, especially when compared with Long Reach or Blackwell depots. This view was confirmed when we arrived half an hour later and pulled into the yard. Notwithstanding the four UniVans we'd passed on the service road going in, and the dozen or so parked on the bay, there was little in the way of proper activity taking place anywhere. Instead, a number of men stood around examining the concrete floor, or looking with deep interest at the steel-span roof. As for vans actually being loaded or unloaded, these amounted to none.

Not that it mattered, of course. Like I said before, it was appearances that counted, and by all appearances this depot was a model of efficiency. As I reversed onto the bay, Bert Hawkes, Merry Park's transport manager, began his daily journey from the main offices to the engineers' workshop, a walk of about seventy yards. This was in order to collect the worksheets for UniVans that had undergone repair during the day, and to return those from the day before. Meanwhile, several drivers helped one another to put their vehicles through the automatic wash (making sure mirrors didn't become misaligned and so forth). The bay itself was almost entirely clear of goods, another sign of efficiency, and the three forklift trucks that waited in attendance had a look of being highly polished and lightly oiled.

In the midst of all this Jonathan and I got out of our van, opened the roller door and prepared to hand over the pallet trolley. Unlike Blackwell, where Len was always on to you in an instant, getting dealt with at Merry Park required a certain amount of patience. I knew from experience that the staff here consisted of two general types. The first category were quite cooperative, helpful even, but also very difficult to find as they spent large parts of the day secluded in the inner recesses of the depot. If you interrupted them in the middle of a card game, for example, they would quite happily lay down their hands to come and unload you. Unfortunately, this required a detailed knowledge of the building, because cards weren't played upstairs in the games room, but in an annex at the rear. These recluses counted among their number such men as Ernie Turner, Kenny Knowles and Mick McVitie.

The other group could always be found somewhere

on the bay, but didn't seem very interested in unloading UniVans (especially after three o'clock when they began sweeping the floor for the evening shutdown). They tended to congregate around a warehouseman called Billy Barker, whom I regarded as a sort of mouthpiece for the rest of them. When we'd first arrived I'd spotted Billy leaning on a broom at the far end of the bay, but now that we were parked with our door open there was no sign of him. Instead, I attempted to catch the eye of one of his sidekicks, an individual known as Beak. He'd become temporarily separated from his friends and was making his way back towards them. When he saw me he tried to dodge behind a forklift, but I intercepted him as he reappeared on the other side. With no further means to elude me, he came to a halt.

'Yes, mate?'

'Are you expecting a pallet trolley?'

'No, mate.'

'Well who is, then?'

'Dunno, mate.'

I wasn't really in the mood to be stonewalled in such a manner, not at this time of day, so I turned towards the super's office and said, 'Alright, I'll have to go and ask Mr Huggins.'

This brought the required change in Beak's demeanour.

'Tell you what,' he said. 'Pull it out and we'll have a look.'

Strictly speaking, it wasn't my job to pull anything out, but I wasn't going to make a fuss on this score so

I obliged and got the trolley onto the bay. As I did so we were joined by Billy Barker, who'd obviously decided to approach us once he'd seen there were no crates to unload.

'Hello,' he said. 'Where's that come from?'

'Cotton Town,' I replied.

'Thought so. That's the one Trevor King shoved over the edge of the bay.'

'How do you know that?'

'Look at the handle,' said Billy. 'It's bent in the middle.'

'Blimey,' I said. 'Trevor King. That's a name from the past. Whatever happened to him?'

'Got the sack, didn't he?'

'Sacked? No one gets sacked from The Scheme.'

'Trevor did.'

'What? For shoving a trolley off the bay?'

'Oh no,' said Billy. 'That was after he'd got the sack.'

'So what did he do that was so bad then?'

'He took a UniVan home for the night.'

'What!'

'It was pouring with rain and he couldn't be bothered walking. He'd have got away with it too if he hadn't come in late the next day. As it was the yard was empty when he finally rolled in at half past eight. He got dismissed on the spot, and took it out on that trolley.'

How much of Billy's story was actually true was hard to tell, but it was enough to break the ice. Ever since we'd arrived at Merry Park, Jonathan had stood by the van looking a little aloof and awkward. Now he joined in the laughter, and appeared more at ease when Billy turned to him with a grin and said, 'Let that be a lesson to you!'

A movement in the yard caught my eye, and I saw Bert Hawkes commence his return journey from the engineers' workshop to the main offices. This meant we'd been at Merry Park for almost twenty minutes and still hadn't got rid of that trolley!

'Right,' I said. 'Who's going to sign for this?'

'Dunno,' said Billy with a shrug. 'Who ordered it?'

'Dunno,' I replied.

'Well, we can't take it then, can we?'

'Why don't I just leave it in a corner somewhere?'

'You're joking,' he said. 'How long you been on The Scheme?'

This question required no answer, of course. With no sign of Huggins (or any other super for that matter), I decided the best course of action was to reload the trolley and take it back to Long Reach. I could always come back another day if anyone decided they wanted it. Four o'clock was approaching. As Billy and his friends continued solemnly sweeping the bay, Jonathan and I prepared to make our departure from Merry Park depot.

'By the way,' I said, when we were back in the cab. 'There's someone over here who's well worth keeping on good terms with.'

I started up and eased the van across the yard towards the gate house. High up, sitting behind his window, I could see John Jones. As usual he was leaning over a newspaper, and showed no apparent sign that he'd noticed our presence.

'Sees everything, John does,' I said. 'Hears all the rumours. Says nothing unless you ask him. Well worth keeping in with.'

To demonstrate my point I bibbed the horn as we passed, hoping John would emerge and exchange some pleasantry for Jonathan's benefit. On this occasion, however, he merely inclined his head by the slightest fraction, and continued reading. Such was the prerogative of a gatekeeper.

'So you're well in with him then, are you?' asked Jonathan.

'Sort of,' I replied.

One advantage of our wasted journey to Merry Park was that we didn't have to worry about getting back to Long Reach prematurely. While other drivers had to scratch around to pass the time, I was able to put my foot down and bomb all the way home along the Ring Road. We enjoyed a good run, rolling through the gates at four fifteen exactly. Naturally the yard was quite busy by this time, with more than a dozen UniVans already backed onto the bay, and the remainder parked opposite. I stopped at the end of the rank, wrote down the daily mileage, and locked up the van. Then Jonathan and I went over to join Ron Curtain, whom I'd noticed standing by his vehicle. There was a large group of drivers, assistant drivers and warehousemen gathered near the super's office, all within striking distance of the clock, but none too close to be obvious.

At eighteen minutes past, however, Bryan Tovey strode forward and clanged the punch bell.

'Goodnight!' he called.

Up in the office, Horsefall was sitting with his back to the door. When he heard the bell he glanced casually at his wristwatch, but otherwise gave no response.

Bryan clanged the bell again.

'Goodnight!'

No response.

The clock ticked round to nineteen minutes past.

Clang.

'Goodnight!'

No response.

Ron shook his head at Bryan's antics. 'You'd think he could come up with something else for a change, wouldn't you?' he remarked. 'We get this performance almost every evening.'

Now Pete Fentiman joined in, clanging the bell and saying 'Goodnight' alternately with Bryan. A buzz of anticipation passed amongst the crowd of spectators, but still the clock seemed reluctant to move beyond four nineteen.

Another clang at last brought Horsefall to the door.

'That'll do!' he rasped, from the top of the steps. 'Four twenty you finish, and not a minute sooner!'

'Sorry,' said Bryan. 'I was just saying goodnight, that's all.'

He now took the liberty of placing his duty card in

the punch, and stood with his hand in readiness above the bell.

'Come on, clock,' he said. 'Get a move on.'

There was a tick, and a cheer rose across the bay.

'Alright,' said Horsefall. 'Off you go.'

A frenzy of activity followed as almost fifty men clocked off for the duty's end. Despite the numbers this was done in a fairly orderly manner because everyone knew who'd got back before them, and who after. There were some cards already in the rack, of course, placed there by the lucky individuals who'd managed to get signed off early. Most of us had to wait our turn, though, and I didn't punch my card until half past four.

'That's why we're allowed our ten-off-the-eight,' I explained to Jonathan. 'Officially it's supposed to be locking-up time, but really it's for clocking off.'

'Is ten-off-the-eight the same as an early bath?' he asked.

'You mean early swerve.'

'Oh yes, sorry. Early swerve.'

'No. It's different. Clocking off's when you have to clock out. Early swerve's when you don't.'

'But I can't clock out anyway,' he said. 'I haven't got a card.'

'No,' I said. 'You're on the same duty as me so we share the card. Once you know what you've got to do we can take turns nicking off at the start of the ten.'

'Oh, I see,' he murmured, a perplexed look on his face. 'I think.'

As Jonathan wandered towards the main gates I

realized he'd had to take quite a lot on board during his first day, what with learning the run and getting to know the various depots, each with their own characteristics. At the same time I knew it wouldn't be long before he got into the swing of things, and that after a few days of going over the same routine he'd begin to get used to it.

Nonetheless, I was quite surprised when I arrived the following morning and found our UniVan waiting on the bay with the engine already running. A quick look in the cab told me that the heater had been switched on and was warming up nicely. Then Jonathan appeared.

'I've seen Arthur for the keys,' he announced. 'So I thought I might as well start her up and park her up.'

'Oh . . . er . . . well done,' I said. 'He gave you the keys alright then, did he?'

'Yes,' said Jonathan. 'No problem. Had quite a nice chat with him actually.'

'What, with Arthur?'

'Yeah.'

'What about?'

'All sorts. He's been on The Scheme since it first started apparently. Says he can tell who's doing what duty by the times the keys come back.'

'That sounds like Arthur.'

'Takes a very dim view of the early swervers, from what I gather.'

'Yes,' I said. 'He's very much a flat-day man.'

'Talking of which,' said Jonathan, flourishing the duty card. 'I've clocked on to save you doing it.'

'Thanks.' I took the card, which he'd partially filled in. 'Do you want to drive the van all day as well?'

The moment I uttered this remark I decided it was churlish and unnecessary. Fortunately Jonathan didn't hear it, because at that moment Chris Darling arrived with a forklift truck.

'Six pallets for you today,' he announced. 'All going to Blackwell.'

'Righto,' answered Jonathan, before I could get a word in. 'That'll keep Len nice and busy.'

Next thing he'd raised the roller door and was supervising Chris as he got the first pallet inside. Feeling slightly surplus to requirements, I went over to the cafe for tea and doughnuts. Sitting at one of the tables, enjoying a full breakfast, was Steve Moore.

'You're cutting it fine, aren't you?' I said. 'You know it's gone eight?'

'That's alright,' Steve replied. 'I've got plenty of time. Care to join me?'

'No thanks. I'll have to go in a sec.'

I glanced at his table. Laid upon it was not only a plate of sausages, eggs, mushrooms, tomatoes, black pudding, baked beans and fried slice, but also bread and butter on a separate plate, a jar of marmalade, toast, tea in a pot, cup-and-saucer, milk, sugar and three different newspapers. Steve looked as if he was there for the duration.

'Alright for some,' I said. 'First I see you coasting up and down the minor roads without a worry in the world, and now here you are with your own private trough, digesting national affairs.'

Steve smiled and stretched himself. 'Well,' he said, with a yawn. 'When you've been on The Scheme as long as I have you deserve the odd privilege now and again.'

'What you doing then?'

'Oh, you know. Bit of this. Bit of that. Making myself useful.'

The self-satisfied way Steve said this made me realize he had no intention of giving away the details of whatever caper he was involved in. For it undoubtedly was a caper. No drivers could sit idly in cafes at eight o'clock in the morning unless they had a legitimate excuse. Steve obviously did have one, but he was giving nothing away. And as for his claim to have earned some privilege through long service, well I knew for a fact that he'd only joined The Scheme about six months before me! I didn't bother saying anything, though, and instead collected my doughnuts and left Steve sitting at the table with a smug expression on his face.

Back on the loading bay, Jonathan was now engaged talking to Horsefall, who'd apparently left the confines of his office and come for one of his 'wanders'. These generally consisted of a nose around the depot, peering into the backs of UniVans and anywhere else that caught his fancy. Remembering we still had the pallet trolley from last week on board, I instinctively went to pull down the roller door, only to discover that Jonathan had already done it.

I looked at the two of them, standing some twenty feet away, and wondered what they could be discussing. Nothing of importance, probably, but it struck me that Jonathan might be one of those new recruits who thought it an advantage to be 'in' with the supers. If so, then he was bound to be disappointed. Oh, I admit Horsefall was a reasonable man, as were many of his colleagues. All the same, I could never understand what drove them to apply for their posts in the first place. I mean to say, they'd only started out as drivers and warehousemen, just like the rest of us. A few of them had even originated in the engineering section, yet they'd chosen to give up their trades in order to preside over others. Put simply, I was of the firm belief that superintendents had different motivations to ordinary employees on The Scheme, and therefore needed to be handled with care.

Having said that, there were occasions when it was important to maintain good relations with them. Before leaving Long Reach I discovered another note from George reminding me about his cakes, which meant that the first thing I had to do when we arrived at Blackwell was to get clearance from Osgood.

'OK to drop off the one cake this afternoon?' I enquired, putting my head round his door.

'Yes,' he replied. 'Should be alright. Stick it under the desk if I'm not here.'

'Righto. Thanks.'

By now, Jonathan's natural inquisitiveness had caused him to become quite interested in the cakes.

'It's just a little sideline of my regular assistant,' I explained, as we got going towards Cotton Town. 'Completely harmless. Just a matter of transferring a few boxes here and there.'

As on the previous day, a dozen cakes needed to be dropped off at Sandro's Bakery, and on our arrival there I was pleased when Jonathan offered to help carry them all in. For his part, Sandro was friendliness itself, insisting that we stayed a few minutes for a cup of tea.

'So, my friend,' he said. 'You've enrolled in our great Scheme for Full Employment?'

'Yes,' replied Jonathan. 'This is my first proper week.'

'Well you have glorious days ahead of you,' declared Sandro. 'Glorious, glorious days.'

As he spoke I was again reminded of the high regard in which The Scheme was held by the public at large. Sandro was the most hard-working man I'd ever met. Every day he spent long hours labouring over hot ovens, along with his three devoted helpers, while we lived a life of ease, cruising around in our vans. Yet he addressed us as if we belonged to some higher order of existence, and had been especially chosen for our destinies.

'Yes,' I remarked. 'We've got nothing to complain about really.'

'Alright, my friends,' said Sandro. 'See you tomorrow.'

He handed me the cake for the onward journey and we said goodbye. For some reason his kitchen had seemed particularly hot this morning, so it was pleasant getting outside again. I paused for a moment to enjoy the cool breeze, and then felt a chill run right through me. Standing by the UniVan was a figure in a black coat, and wearing a black peaked cap.

'Oh no,' I murmured. 'It's Nesbitt.'

'Who's that then?' asked Jonathan, obviously aware of my guarded tone.

'Gold Badge,' I said. 'Let me do the talking.'

Nesbitt wasn't looking in our direction, but I had no doubt he was fully aware of our approach. He stood staring at the van's front nearside wheel, motionless as we walked up.

'Morning, Mr Nesbitt,' I ventured.

'Morning,' he replied, without raising his eyes. 'Glad you've come back. It's a bit parky waiting here.'

'Yes, I suppose it must be.'

'So let's all get in the cab, shall we?'

'Right.'

With the cake box seeming very conspicuous under my arm, I fumbled for the keys in my pocket. Then I unlocked the door, put the cake inside, and turned to find Nesbitt's gaze upon me.

'That's a funny blue.'

5

'What is?' I asked.

'Your shirt.'

'But it's regulation blue collar.'

Nesbitt tucked his chin into his neck and regarded me from beneath his peak.

'It may be blue collar,' he said. 'But it's not regulation.'

'It used to be.'

'Yes, well I used to be a babe-in-arms. That shirt belongs to last year, so get rid of it and remove a fresh one from its nice cellophane wrapper. You received your new issue, I take it?'

'Yes.'

'Right then. I'll expect you to be wearing it next time I see you.'

'OK.'

'I won't take the matter any further, considering it's the season of goodwill.'

'Thanks.'

'Now let's get in out of the cold.'

In one movement, Nesbitt stepped towards the UniVan and swung up into the dummy seat, closing the door behind him. I walked round to the driver's side, followed by Jonathan.

'Season of goodwill?' I said, lowering my voice. 'What's he talking about? That was weeks ago.'

Nesbitt wasn't a particularly large man, but when I opened my door and looked in he seemed to fill the far side of the cab with his presence. Still wearing his peaked cap, complete with glinting Gold Badge, he sat gazing through the windscreen, waiting for us to join him. There was barely room for Jonathan, but he had to get in all the same, scrambling across behind the wheel and ending up perched on the metal cowling in the middle. He was in for an uncomfortable journey. Then I got in beside him and shut my door.

'Thought I'd have a little ride round with you,' Nesbitt announced. 'It's a while since I've visited these parts, so I want to refresh my memory. Just carry on as if I wasn't here please.'

'We're going to Cotton Town next,' I said, trying to sound helpful.

'Yes,' he replied. 'I'm quite aware of that.'

I started up and pulled the UniVan out into the traffic, hoping the noise of the engine would save us from having to hold a conversation with Nesbitt. For the time being it did, and all three of us sat in mute silence as we sped along the Ring Road. Now and again I glanced at the cake box, lying on top of the dashboard immediately in front of Nesbitt and partially blocking his line of vision. As Jonathan had mentioned on his first day, it was prohibited to carry goods in the cab, but so far nothing had been said. I tried not to think about this too much, and concentrated my mind on getting to Cotton Town at the scheduled time. This I achieved, rolling through the main gates at twelve forty-five exactly.

It was interesting to see the effect that our arrival had on the depot staff. As we entered the yard Hoskins was standing in his favourite spot, timing everyone in for dinner. He nodded casually as our vehicle passed him by, then practically stood to attention when he saw who was sitting in the dummy seat. Similarly, activity on the loading bay seemed to double when I reversed in and Nesbitt opened his door. Kevin Jennings appeared in an instant, whistling heartily as he manoeuvred his forklift into a ready position behind the UV. Kevin's strident tunelessness alerted Cliff Clifford, who entered the scene moments later pushing an extra-wide broom in front of him. It also brought Watts to his office door. He emerged as Nesbitt came up the steps from the yard.

'Ah, hello, Cyril,' he said, clearly taken by surprise. 'What brings you to this neck of the woods?'

'Curiosity,' replied Nesbitt. 'Got a lift from these gentlemen.'

Thus thrown into the spotlight Jonathan and I both made ourselves look busy. I'd brought with me the latest batch of dockets, so I began leafing through them to find one headed Cotton Town. Meanwhile, Jonathan undid the catch and slid open the roller door, revealing the pallet trolley we'd been carrying around for almost a week.

A moment passed during which I looked up to see Jonathan glance at me, then back at the trolley. Kevin looked at the trolley, then at me. Watts looked at Kevin, then the trolley, then me. No one looked at Nesbitt.

'Something the matter?' he asked.

'Er . . . no, no,' replied Watts. 'Quite a light loading today, isn't there?'

'Yes,' I answered, taking up the cue. 'We had quite a lot for Blackwell, though.'

'Really?'

'Yes.'

'But nothing for us?'

'No. That trolley's on its way to Merry Park.'

'Oh,' said Watts, giving me a long look. 'I see.'

Our leaden exchange of words ceased when Nesbitt suddenly stepped inside the UniVan. We watched as he ran a familiar hand over the trolley's brake bar.

'This reminds me of the old days,' he said. 'Before we went electric.'

Needless to say, Nesbitt's pronouncement wasn't a signal for a cosy chat about some former golden age. Instead its purpose was to remind all present of his seniority, and therefore his authority, over the rest of us. Not that we needed such a reminder. Kevin, Cliff and myself were fully aware of his reputation, and we knew that even Watts, a mere Silver Badge official, needed to watch his p's and q's when Nesbitt was around. Addressing him as 'Cyril', for example, had been a calculated risk. Hoskins, meanwhile, maintained a polite silence. Jonathan was the only person who had no idea of the importance of a Gold Badge, but nonetheless he appeared to be overawed by the man in the black peaked cap.

After several moments of staring at the trolley in quiet contemplation, Nesbitt turned to Kevin.

'Got anything for Blackwell?' he asked.

'Just two pallets,' Kevin replied.

Nesbitt glanced at his wristwatch.

'Ten to one,' he said. 'Plenty of time.'

Without another word he led the way towards the office, followed closely by Watts, while Kevin and the rest of us made a big show of loading the two pallets onto the UniVan in an efficient manner. At three minutes to one the task was complete, but there was no question of sloping off for dinner. Instead we each seized a broom and gave the bay yet another sweep. Only at one o'clock was it safe to stop work. Cliff and Kevin downed tools on the dot and headed for the canteen doors.

'Go with them and meet a few people,' I urged Jonathan. 'Have a round of cards; they're all quite friendly.'

'Are you coming?' he asked.

'No,' I said. 'Think I'll stay with the van.'

I spent the next half-hour wondering what to do about the cake. It sat there on top of the dashboard like a piece of damning evidence, a signpost advertising the fact that we'd broken one of the cardinal rules of The Scheme. The conveyance of private goods by UniVan, either in the cab or in the back, was not allowed, and if I had any sense I'd get rid of it there and then. On the other hand, Nesbitt had made no mention of the box during our journey to Cotton Town, which suggested he'd chosen to ignore it. The only way I could get it passed on to Pete Giggs was by taking it to Blackwell depot, so finally I decided I would stick to the plan and hope for the best.

A secondary line of thought concerned Watts, and his reaction when he saw the pallet trolley. I'd always had Watts down as an unbending authoritarian, but now I realized I'd misjudged him. He could easily have dropped me right in it for not getting that trolley delivered, especially with Nesbitt present, yet he'd actually gone out of his way to change the subject. I made a mental note that Watts was a softer touch than I'd previously thought. It was always useful knowing these things.

Nesbitt, though, was completely unfathomable. Osgood had remarked that no one knew how his mind worked, but really this was a profound understatement. Nesbitt was a totally free agent whose sole duty was to perpetuate the smooth running of The Scheme. A man with unlimited powers, he investigated anything that caught his fancy, and today, for reasons of his own, he'd decided to ride round in our UniVan. I expected him to come back at exactly one thirty, so at twenty-five past I got behind the wheel and waited. In the event it was Jonathan who returned first.

'I overheard some interesting discussions up in the canteen,' he said. 'In fact, there were a few heated arguments.'

'What about?' I asked.

'Well, there was a table by me and they were talking about the best way to get an early swerve.'

'Oh yes?'

'One bloke said you just had to go slow all day until you were so far behind schedule that they had to sign your card. Then this other bloke said he was wrong, and that the best approach was to get in with a particular super, so you could get a signature in advance. But the first bloke didn't like that because it meant you owed them a favour.'

'True.'

'They were just going on and on about finishing early, as if their whole day was built around it.'

'It is, for some of them.'

'But I thought this was supposed to be The Scheme for Full Employment!'

'Yeah . . .'

'Well, I can't see how it can be if no one's got enough to do.'

'The point is,' I said, 'there's a difference between full employment and being fully employed. True, there is a lot of spare capacity in The Scheme, but it's better for people to be paid to do very little than have no job at all, isn't it?'

'Suppose.'

'You're right, though,' I conceded. 'Some of them do tend to take the early swerve thing a bit far.'

'That's exactly what this other bloke told them. John, his name was, I think. He suddenly came marching up to the table and said they were going to ruin everything if they carried on the way they were.'

'That'll be John Ford,' I said. 'He's a great believer in The Scheme, but also highly opinionated.'

'Well, he had a real go at the others.'

'And what did they say back to him?'

'They just laughed.'

The nearside door opened and Nesbitt peered in.

'Who laughed?' he asked.

'Er . . . some people up in the canteen,' replied Jonathan.

'Good,' said Nesbitt. 'Glad to hear everybody's happy. Move over, can you.'

While talking to me, Jonathan had been lolling in the dummy seat, seemingly forgetful of Nesbitt's imminent return. Now, he was once again obliged to find a perch on the centre cowling. Then Nesbitt got in and we continued our daily round.

During the next part of the journey it struck me how quickly we'd adapted to having such an important passenger on board. Apart from putting a stop to all but the most necessary talk, his presence had also affected the way I was driving. There was a code of conduct on The Scheme that included courtesy to other road-users. This was wrapped up with the image of the Uni-

Van as a sort of model, skilfully-driven vehicle, sharing the highways with everybody else. The reality, of course, was different. Due to their size and sluggishness, UniVans were in fact the primary cause of traffic congestion in most towns and cities, and this often brought out the worst in fellow drivers. It was a common sight to see a UV being carved up by some car or lorry, desperate to get in front. The result was that we all tended to defend our road space quite robustly, as if we were in command of assault tanks rather than humble utility vehicles. Today, however, I was courtesy personified. Under Nesbitt's scrutiny I became the politest, most considerate person ever to sit behind a steering wheel, giving way to all and sundry, and beckoning over-takers with a cheery wave of the hand. Nesbitt passed no comment on any of this, nor did he look anywhere except at the road dead ahead. Nonetheless, I knew he was clocking my every move.

Fatigue was beginning to set in by the time we arrived at Blackwell. Normally, this would be the opportunity for a cup of tea, but I had a feeling that today we would be missing out. One thing was for certain, though: the depot had been forewarned that Nesbitt was coming. This was evident from the number of staff who materialized on the bay the moment we entered the yard. From what I could see it was practically a full complement. Charlie Green and Mick Dalston were busy tidying up a huge stack of surplus pallets, assisted by Dennis Clark and Steve Carter. Meanwhile, Len Walker was occupied getting his forklift truck into position. As

I reversed in, Gosling descended from the office and began guiding me back with a series of meaningless hand signals. This actually made the manoeuvre more difficult than usual. I'd been driving UniVans for five years, yet because of Gosling I only made it squarely onto the bay at my second attempt. At last I switched off the engine and waited for Nesbitt to get out. Instead, he remained sitting exactly where he was.

'Now then,' he said. 'We seem to have an additional item on board.'

He was looking directly at the cake box.

'Oh,' I said. 'Yes.'

'So let's have a look inside, shall we?'

Nesbitt reached forward, lifted the box off the dashboard and placed it on top of his knees. Then he removed the lid. Inside was a cake covered with yellow icing. It had a circle of crystallized oranges and lemons round the outside, and on top was a tiny sugar bicycle, as well as some candles and the words: FOR A VERY SPECIAL BOY WHO'S FIVE TODAY.

'Rather pretty,' remarked Nesbitt. 'Has it got marzipan in it?'

'Should think so,' I replied.

'I'm very partial to a bit of marzipan.'

'Are you?'

'Very partial indeed.'

For a few moments I remembered my own distant childhood, and the weeks I used to spend waiting for my birthday to come round. I recalled that on those far-gone occasions the candlelit cake had always been central to my boyish hopes and dreams, the guarantee that there would be many happy returns of the day.

Then I turned to Nesbitt and said, 'Like a slice?'

'Yes, thank you,' he said. 'It'll go down nicely with a cup of tea.'

Replacing the lid, he put the box under his arm and got out of the UniVan. Jonathan and I looked at each other, and followed after him.

'Afternoon, Cyril!' called Osgood from the office door. 'I've got the kettle on if you'd care to partake.'

If Osgood realized what Nesbitt was carrying with him he didn't show it. Professional that he was, he simply stood holding the door open as his superior mounted the steps and went inside. Gosling, I noticed, was not invited to join them.

Len Walker seemed positively delighted about Nesbitt's visit.

'Heh heh!' he kept saying. 'There'll be no one getting away early today.'

Certainly, Charlie and the rest of them appeared to have accepted this as an unavoidable fact. Having completely rebuilt their stack of pallets, they next directed their energies into unloading a van that had arrived after me. The swiftness with which they went about the task surprised the driver and his assistant, who came sauntering onto the bay to find the process already in full motion. Informed of Nesbitt's presence, however, they soon fell into line and set about giving their mirrors and headlights an extensive polish.

All this activity gave Gosling something to concentrate on, and he seemed moderately happy overseeing operations during the fifteen minutes or so that the office door remained closed. When it opened again we were all busily engaged in our respective duties. Nesbitt emerged with the cake box tucked under his arm.

I had been half-hoping he would choose to spend the rest of the afternoon at Blackwell, especially after Len's remark that no one would be getting away early. Surely, I thought, he must have had enough by now of riding round in a UniVan. But I was wrong. Still carrying the box, he descended the stairs and headed back towards our vehicle. As Jonathan and I trailed after him we received pitying glances from the others. Osgood stood in his doorway, looking thoroughly relieved that Nesbitt's sojourn was over.

Back in the cab, I saw the cake box sitting on top of the dashboard as though it had never been moved. Jonathan was balanced on his perch, while Nesbitt sat leafing through his schedules book.

'Right,' he said. 'You're due to go to Merry Park now.'

'Yes,' I replied. 'Last call of the day.'

Nesbitt closed the book and slipped it into his pocket.

'Well, I'm not minded to go to Merry Park,' he announced. 'You haven't picked up from here, have you?'

'No, there wasn't anything.'

'Right you are. Give me your duty card and I'll sign you straight back to Long Reach. Then we can all get home a bit sooner, can't we?'

'Er . . . yes,' I said, handing him the card. 'Thanks.'

'It's not a matter of thanks,' he said. 'It's a matter of I've got a long way to go.'

While Nesbitt was writing the details, I suddenly remembered I hadn't exchanged dockets with Len for the two pallets we'd delivered. The simple ritual had been forgotten in the midst of all the frenetic activity, so I got out of the van and went to find him. When I came back about three minutes later, Nesbitt was still holding the card, but now seemed to be examining it more closely. It was our final week on that duty, so most of the spaces were filled in.

'Seem to be a lot of signatures on here,' Nesbitt remarked. 'Looks as though you've hardly been to Merry Park this last month.'

'No,' I answered. 'Suppose not.'

'And it's always the same person who's signed it.'

'Yes.'

'Wednesday, Thursday and Friday last week. Monday, Tuesday the week before. Friday the week before that. Whose name's this then?'

I took the card and ran my eyes over an identical series of signatures. Each consisted of a letter g with a long extended tail.

'Er . . . it belongs to Mr Gosling, I think.'

'Mr Gosling,' repeated Nesbitt, taking back the card. 'I see.'

He reached into the inner recesses of his coat and produced a book. For a moment I thought this must be the book of schedules he'd been studying earlier, but one glance told me its pages were blank. Next thing, Nesbitt was copying particulars from our duty card, underneath which he wrote various comments of his own. Then he put the book away again.

'Alright,' he said. 'Let's go to Long Reach.'

6

When I walked into the duty room next morning, Bob Little called me over to the counter.

'Don't bother clocking in,' he said. 'Ray Coppin wants to see you.'

'Do you know what it's about?' I asked.

'No, I don't,' replied Bob. 'He just said could you go up at eight o'clock.'

'Alright then. Is someone covering my duty?'

'Yes, we've asked Peter Lawrence to do it.'

'Oh, right.'

This was the first time Ray had ever asked to see me, and I had no idea what he wanted me for. I only hoped it had nothing to do with Nesbitt. Before I went upstairs, however, I had to go and remove the cake box from our vehicle. Peter Lawrence was a bloke who did the job dead straight, and I knew he'd want no involvement with George's cakes. He was also the sort of man who turned in early for work, and when I found him he already had the van unlocked with the engine running. Jonathan was standing with him looking slightly bewildered.

'I've got to go and see the depot manager,' I explained. 'Don't worry: Peter'll look after you alright.'

'You in trouble then?' Peter asked.

'Don't think so,' I said. 'But you never can tell for sure. Look, I just need to take something out of the cab. See you later.'

'Yes, see you,' he said. 'Come on, Jonathan. We'd better get a cup of tea before we go.'

I decided the best thing to do with the box was leave it with Rob Marshall in the engineers' workshop. On my way there I lifted the lid and had a look inside. The cake was in perfect condition, except that about one fifth was now missing. The tiny sugar bicycle was untouched. When I arrived at the workshop I saw another six boxes on the bench, waiting to be taken away. There was no sign of Rob, so I added yesterday's box to the stack along with an apologetic note to George. Then I took the stairs up to the main offices.

It was a long time since I'd trodden the cold tiles that led to Ray Coppin. He was a hands-off type of manager, fairly popular with the staff, whom we rarely caught sight of. His room was at the end of a wide corridor, along one side of which ran the famous Long Reach mural.

Painted in bright colours, this depicted scenes from daily life on The Scheme. In one section, UniVans were shown being loaded and unloaded by industrious men in smart blue uniforms. In another, they were seen motoring along a great uncluttered highway where the traffic consisted entirely of UniVans. Further images showed dignified superintendents, smiling ancillary staff and resolute gatekeepers, all working together in a spirit of cooperation. The centrepiece was an eight-hour clock beneath a golden scroll. This bore the words: LABOR OMNIBUS.

As I walked the mural's length, the same thought occurred to me as had the last time I'd seen it, namely, that the UniVans it pictured looked different from those in real life. A few slight discrepancies, for example, in the thickness of the windscreen divider, or in the curve of the mudguard, made these vehicles appear much more angular than the ones I was familiar with. The result was that they seemed as if they belonged to another age altogether. Also, the men's arms were much thicker than would be natural. I blamed this on the artist, whose illegible signature appeared in the corner at the far end of the mural.

On the opposite wall was a framed photograph of the UniVan's late designer, Sir Ronald Thompson, wearing spectacles and looking very austere in black-and-white. Vaguely I wondered if he'd ever seen the mural, and what he would have thought of it. Then I came to an office door with a brass plate that said:

I knocked once.

'Come in.'

When I went inside, Ray was standing with his back to his desk looking out of the window. This gave him a fine view over the lower rear roof of the depot, an aspect obscured only by the ventilation stack which stuck up at one side.

'Ah,' he said, when he saw me. 'Thanks for coming in. Take a seat, please.'

I sat down while he went to a nearby cabinet and retrieved a file. Then he settled opposite me.

'Right then,' he began. 'Just one or two questions first. How long have you been on The Scheme?'

'About five years,' I replied.

'And how are you enjoying it so far?'

'Fine thanks.'

'That's good.' Ray leaned back in his chair and put his hands behind his head. 'Yes, I think we've got a happy depot here. Everyone knows what they have to do and the bulk of the work always gets done. Oh, we may not be the height of efficiency, but all in all the fleet's in good order and our rate of flow is easily above the average. Yes, I can safely say we're a very happy depot.'

No sooner had Ray started than I recognized this introductory talk as the one he'd given me on my first day as a new recruit. As a matter of fact it was the one he gave everybody, and was supposed to offer a sort of fatherly reassurance to newcomers. On that earlier occasion he'd gone on to explain the policy of eight hours' work for eight hours' pay, and to inform me I could look forward to glorious days ahead. This morning, however, he soon began to pursue a completely different line.

'Now as you know,' he said, 'The Scheme continues to go from strength to strength. UniVans travel around in their thousands every day, moving goods and maintaining a steady throughput. Nevertheless, there still remain gaps in the network where certain regions have yet to be fully incorporated. The process of integration has been a slow one, but at long last it's arrived at our doorstep.' Ray reached for his file and opened it. 'Have you ever heard of Eden Lacy?'

'Just once,' I replied. 'It's the name of a depot, isn't it?'

'Correct,' said Ray. 'It's one of a few we wish to encompass within our circuit.'

'Oh, right.'

'Obviously we need to prepare the schedules beforehand, and that's where you come in. We've got a little task for you, if you're interested.'

'What would I be doing?'

'We'd like you to drive a UniVan to Eden Lacy, see how long it takes to get there, then come back.'

'How far is it?'

'We've got it as thirty-one miles as the crow flies,' said Ray. 'But that doesn't allow for traffic conditions, gyratory systems and unscheduled stoppages. We need someone to clock the average journey time over a number of successive days. It'd be a job-and-finish, of course.'

'Would it?'

'Oh yes. Do your return trip and the rest of the day's your own.'

'Well, thanks,' I said. 'Yes, I would be very interested.'

'One thing though,' he said, leafing through the file again. 'I've been having a look at your daily mileage reports for December.' Now he was holding a duty card in his hand. 'According to this you did sixty-three miles on Wednesday the fourth, sixty-three miles on Thursday the fifth, and on Friday the sixth, one million, twelve thousand and twenty-two miles. Where did you go that day?'

Ray handed me the card so that I could see it for myself. The entry in question was in George's handwriting.

'That should say sixty-three miles,' I said. 'Sorry, we must have put it down wrong.'

'Alright,' said Ray. 'Well, I think it's an oversight that can be overlooked under the circumstances. Try to fill it in more accurately in future.'

'OK, then. Sorry.'

He rose from behind his desk. 'So you'd like to do that little job for us, would you?'

'Yes please.'

'Right you are,' he said. 'You can start this morning and carry on for ten days or so, until you've got an average. Pop and see the engineers for a spare vehicle.'

81

'Thanks.' I stood up to leave, and then thought of something else I wanted to ask.

'Can I enquire why you chose me?'

'Yes, you can,' replied Ray. 'Your name was pulled out of a hat.'

'Oh.'

At that moment the phone rang and he picked it up. 'Ray Coppin speaking. Oh yes, that would be perfect. Can I have orange marmalade today please, and some egg soldiers, and could you make sure the eggs are nice and fluffy . . .'

Ray was still ordering breakfast as I showed myself out.

The first person I saw when I got down to the yard was Steve Moore. He was lounging against his UniVan with a newspaper spread before him. As I appeared from the direction of the stairway he gave me a knowing look.

'Is that what you've been doing this last couple of weeks?' I asked. 'Timing runs?'

'Yep,' he grinned. 'Here to Royal Pond and back. Cushy little number.'

'So why were you being so secretive?'

'Didn't want to make anyone jealous, did I?' Steve folded his paper. 'Coming over to the cafe for some *petit déjeuner*?'

'No, thanks,' I said. 'I've got to get a van sorted out and everything.'

'Don't think I'll bother leaving till ten o'clock,' he announced. 'Nice round figure. See you on the road then.'

'Yes, see you.'

When I walked into the engineers' workshop, Rob Marshall was gazing at the stack of cake boxes on his bench.

'What am I going to do with this lot?'

'Don't know,' I said. 'But I'm sure you'll find a solution. You engineers always do. Is Ken around?'

'Who wants him?' said a voice from the inner office.

'Me,' I replied. 'Ray Coppin's asked me to do a timing run, so I need a van for ten days.'

Ken Scanlon emerged and remarked, 'Ah, one of the chosen few. Just a moment please.' Ken was chief engineer, and responsible for the allocation of vehicles. Referring to a wall chart, he said, 'UV61's free. You can take that one.'

'Thanks.'

He nodded towards the cakes. 'Your assistant's taking a liberty, isn't he?'

'Suppose so.'

'I think I'll have to start demanding a percentage.'

'You might as well,' I said. 'Nesbitt's already had his cut.'

Before I could do anything with UV61 I had to see Arthur for the keys. It took a few minutes to get him to come to his hatch, and when he did he complained that it was 'highly irregular' to give keys out to anyone after eight o'clock. He eventually handed them over, however, and then I went to the duty room to get a regional map from Bob Little. These had been introduced as guides to new drivers, but in practice nobody bothered with them. As a result they lay unused and yellowing on a shelf under the counter. Each map was printed on a thin sheet of paper, with dotted lines showing how to fold it correctly. I ignored these, and folded mine first into quarters, then eighths.

Opening it out again, I spread it on a table and perused it closely. All the depots in the region were shown as a letter D enclosed in a square, along with an identifying name. The size of the square indicated the capacity of the depot. As a result, places such as Merry Park, Blackwell and our own Long Reach stood out as important landmarks, whereas the much smaller Rudgeway, for example, took a little longer to locate.

As for Eden Lacy, well for a while I couldn't find it at all. I studied the tangle of roads, canals and railways until my eyes were beginning to feel the strain, but it simply failed to stand out. I was just beginning to think the map-makers had forgotten to include it when right at the top I saw a tiny square with a letter D inside. Also were the words: EDEN LACY.

I wasn't a bit surprised to discover it was situated in the far north of the region, as the name had that sort of ring about it. It was certainly much further away than any of the other depots shown, and looked rather isolated compared to the rest of them. Moreover, there appeared to be no direct route to Eden Lacy. Instead, it only seemed approachable along a series of minor roads. Immediately I realized that my hopes of cruising along some smooth unbroken thoroughfare were not about to be met. Nonetheless, the chance of a lengthy solo journey in a UniVan, following a schedule of my own making, was highly attractive. I borrowed a marker pen from Bob and traced out the shortest distance to Eden Lacy. Then I went to seek out UV61.

All the UniVans were supposedly identical. They were constructed from the same interchangeable components, and in theory could only be distinguished by their fleet numbers. There should have been no difference between UV61 and, say, UV55, the van I'd been using the day before. In reality, though, every vehicle had its own particular characteristics. Some steered better than others, some were faster, some were more rattly. What made UV61 unique was its very soft suspension, a fact I remembered with glee as I unlocked the cab and slid behind the wheel. I'd driven 61 on many previous occasions, and I knew it would be perfect for an excursion like this. With nothing to load or unload, I was free to leave at once.

The route I'd worked out required me to go west along the Ring Road for about five miles before turning north. In this first part of the trip I encountered several UniVans, some coming towards Long Reach, others making their way to more distant destinations. Those drivers who knew me flashed their lights in recognition, just as they always did. I flashed back, but for some reason I found their attentions rather irritating. Why this was I couldn't explain, since we all flashed each other as a matter of course. This morning, however, the vans that came plodding along on their daily round looked very ordinary, and their crews appeared hidebound and unadventurous. In contrast, I was engaged on a mission that promised to be most interesting. Consequently, I soon stopped acknowledging oncoming vehicles, and pressed on as if I hadn't seen them. This became easier once I'd turned off and headed north. From now on the vans I passed were largely driven by strangers. I'd seen some of them before, of course, at depots like Merry Park, where several circuits overlapped, and had even said hello to one or two. But the sheer immensity of The Scheme meant that it was impossible to be on familiar terms with more than a handful of other drivers. Soon I was seeing UniVans with unknown identification plates. Mine bore the letters LR (for Long Reach), and I saw a couple displaying CG, which indicated they were based at Castle Gate. The majority, though, could have come from anywhere, with plates that said TT, BN, or, in one case, X. At no point on the journey did I see a vehicle that originated from Eden Lacy. As a matter of fact, my sightings of all UniVans became rarer the further I got from the Ring Road.

After an hour's travel I was still in the conurbation, but in an area where derelict buildings and abandoned ground seemed quite common. It was the sort of wasteland I'd imagined to have been widespread in the days before The Scheme, and which I thought had been eradicated. As I drove on I realized there was still much to be done. Presumably this explained why the process of integration was being stepped up. Ray Coppin had said that certain regions were 'yet to be fully incorporated', and now I'd seen for myself exactly what he meant. Continuing towards my destination, I felt glad to be playing a part, however small, in such a glorious undertaking.

I was within a mile of Eden Lacy when it occurred to me that I hadn't recorded my departure time from Long Reach, and that therefore this first run was invalidated. For a moment I considered simply guessing how long the trip had taken, but that would have made the entire exercise pointless, so instead I decided to regard this as an exploratory journey only. There would be plenty of opportunity over the next ten days to establish an average time.

It was a shiny sort of morning and the road surface gleamed. I'd been on a single carriageway for a fair while now, with hardly anything at all in the way of traffic. After another minute a sign appeared with an arrow pointing to the left. Now I was on a narrow concrete drive, dead straight, with a waterworks on one side, and what appeared to be a brickyard on the other. Directly ahead of me was the depot, and as I drew nearer I saw that there were three men standing on the loading bay, watching my approach. They were all in a row, side by side, and looked as if they'd been waiting there for hours. One of them was quite plump. He stood with his hands thrust deep in the pockets of his blue overalls.

There was no gatehouse here. Instead, the driveway just opened out into a wide and empty yard. At one end was a smaller, open-fronted building which I took to be the engineers' workshop. Inside, perched on a set of ramps, was a lone UniVan. I pulled up in the middle of the open space, and then reversed onto the bay. Still the three men remained motionless. I could see them in my mirror, gazing silently at my vehicle as I backed in. Only when I got out to say hello did they come to life.

'We heard someone might be coming out from Long Reach,' said the plump one, as I came up the steps from the yard.

'Yes,' I replied. 'I'm going to be doing some timing runs over the next few days.'

'That's what we heard.'

Out of habit I went to the van, flipped the catch, and slid open the roller door, revealing the bare interior.

'You haven't got anything for us, have you?' he asked.

'No,' I replied.

'Didn't think you would have.'

'And you won't have anything for me either.'

'No,' he said. 'We only send stuff to Long Reach once a month, and it's always picked up by a van from River-head.'

'Where's that then?'

'Don't know. He only comes once a month.'

I glanced around the depot and saw that there were no laden pallets anywhere. A stack of empty ones stood in the far corner, and beside them waited a forklift truck. It didn't look as though it was used very often. The plump man, I noticed, hadn't removed his hands from his pockets since my arrival.

'Want a cup of tea?'

'Oh, yes please,' I said. 'I'm parched. Canteen upstairs, is it?'

'We haven't got a canteen here. The cleaner makes us tea in the morning, but she's gone home now. We have to do it ourselves. Go and put the kettle on, will you Martin?'

He was addressing one of the other men, who looked like a younger, slightly less portly version of himself, and who could easily have been his son.

'Alright,' said this one, turning to me. 'Do you want sugar?' He had a very high-pitched voice.

'No thanks.'

'You'd better tell Jim,' added the plump man.

'Alright.'

The younger man went to a telephone attached to the wall and picked up the receiver. A moment later we heard a bell ringing over in the workshop. Then it stopped again.

'Jim?' he said into the phone. 'It's Martin. We're making a cup of tea, if you're interested. Right you are. See you in five minutes.'

He hung up and went to put the kettle on. I closed the roller door.

'How many vans have you got here?' I enquired.

'One,' replied the plump man. He nodded across the yard towards the workshop. 'It's being maintained at the present.'

The third member of the trio was a quiet man who smiled a lot but said little. For this reason he struck me as the sort of person it must be nice to have around. His name, I soon discovered, was Eric. The plump man was called Harold. While the arrangements for the tea were being made Eric busied himself with a broom, sweeping the bay along its entire length. The clock by the office told me it was now twelve noon. Surely, I thought, they can't already be clearing up for the day? Not this early. My question was answered almost immediately.

'Here's the Bell Tower,' announced Harold.

Coming up the concrete drive was a UniVan, and next moment it was sweeping into the yard with a loud hoot of its horn. As the vehicle reversed back onto the loading bay I looked at its identification plate. The letters BT confirmed that it was indeed from Bell Tower depot, and instantly a wave of disappointment passed through me. Up until now I'd thought I was the only person from our region ever to visit Eden Lacy. Certainly it had all the feeling of a remote satellite compared to my regular destinations. The greeting given to the new arrivals, however, told me I was by no means the first. When the driver and his assistant got out it was obvious they knew the staff here quite well. Actually, I recognized them myself, having seen them on the circuit occasionally.

'Now then, Keith,' said Harold. 'You're just in time for tea.'

'That makes a change,' came the reply. 'We had to wait ten minutes yesterday!'

When this Keith got to the top of the steps he stopped, looked at me, and said, 'I know your face. Long Reach, isn't it?'

'Yes,' I replied. 'I'm doing a few timing runs.'

'Oh, that's right,' he nodded. 'I heard they were establishing direct contact between here and there.'

His assistant, meanwhile, went to the back of their van and slid open the roller door. There was a polite 'beep' behind me. Eric had abandoned his broom and was now seated in readiness on the forklift truck, still smiling.

In the next few minutes, any thoughts I'd had that this might be a 'sleepy' depot were quickly banished. Keith's vehicle contained six fully-laden pallets, but Eric was so deft at handling the forklift that it was empty in no time. Harold's contribution was to keep out of Eric's way while at the same time appearing busy. He managed this because, despite being plump, he was also very light-footed. With his hands lodged firmly in his pockets, he dodged around inside the UniVan, performing bits of fancy footwork as Eric manoeuvred the goods.

While all this was going on, Martin returned with

a tray of tea and placed it on a table in the corner of the building, around which were several chairs. At the same time another man came strolling across from the direction of the workshop. This I took to be Jim the engineer, whom Martin had called on the phone. When the unloading was complete and the dockets exchanged, everybody gravitated towards the table. Now, for the first time since my arrival, Harold removed his hands from his pockets. They were plump like the rest of him, and in one of them he held a pack of cards.

'Shall we have a quick game?' he asked.

'Might as well,' replied Keith. 'While we're all here.'

The tea was poured, we sat down, and the cards were dealt.

'Whose turn is it to start?'

'Mine,' said Harold. He peered long and hard at his hand of cards, then gave me an enquiring look. 'Have you got Mr Bun the Baker?'

7

By the time I left Eden Lacy, about two hours later, I'd
come to the conclusion it was a thoroughly nice depot.
Nothing was too much trouble for Harold and his companions, who treated their visitors as honoured guests.
After the cards, Martin was dispatched to make some
sandwiches and more tea, while Jim gave mine and
Keith's vehicles a quick once-over in case there were
any 'unwanted oil leaks' as he put it. There weren't, of
course, as the standard of maintenance throughout
The Scheme was always high. Nonetheless, the gesture
was fully appreciated. Jim was an engineer of the tra-
ditional school, with a clean rag in his left pocket, and
an adjustable spanner in his right. He paid a particular
interest in UV61, remarking that it was one of the few
models in the series that he hadn't spotted before. He

opened the bonnet and for a few moments we stood gazing at the engine in solemn reverence.

'Look at that,' he said. 'What a marvellous creation.'

Keith, who was standing just to one side, gave me a wink as Jim closed the lid again. He and Rodney, his assistant driver, both appeared most satisfied with life on The Scheme, and clearly enjoyed their trips to Eden Lacy. They even had their own drinking mugs at the table. All the same, I was surprised how long they remained there, playing cards and generally taking it easy. If they weren't careful, I thought, they were going to get booked for leaving late. I gave a quick glance towards the super's office, and at the very same moment it dawned on me why this depot seemed so relaxed. There weren't any supers here! The office was closed up, with a couple of spare brooms leaning against the door as if they belonged there permanently. Next to the office was the punch clock, with four time-cards resting in the rack above: the only evidence of any link with officialdom. When I asked Harold about this he explained that instead of having supers permanently attached to the depot, they received occasional 'snap' visits instead, when someone like Nesbitt would turn up unannounced.

'Isn't that a bit worrying?' I enquired.

'Course not,' he replied. 'Our driveway's as straight as a die. We can see anyone coming a mile off.'

Apparently there were a few clerks who worked in the main offices at the back of the building, and also a depot manager, but Harold assured me that none of them ever interfered in the day-to-day running of the place. As we sat down to a plateful of Martin's sandwiches, I had to agree that they had everything functioning perfectly.

'These are delicious,' I said. 'Have you ever thought of going into catering?'

'Yes, I've considered it,' replied Martin. 'But I'd probably just eat them all myself.'

Keith and Rodney left at two o'clock, bound for Merry Park. According to Harold, there was a van due at two thirty that would take away some of the pallets they'd just delivered. The rest would be collected at twenty to four. With appropriate haste the three warehousemen began checking through the items in readiness: Martin doing the counting, Eric marking the goods, and Harold standing nearby with his hands in his pockets. Meanwhile I got into my UniVan and headed back to Long Reach, giving them a hoot as I pulled out of the yard.

On my journey to Eden Lacy I'd been concentrating on taking the correct route, but now I knew the road a bit better I had the opportunity to make certain informal observations. Halfway home, for example, I took note of a cafe called Jimmy's, an establishment which looked highly suitable for drivers in search of a late breakfast. Further along were The Cavendish Tea Rooms, which on first impressions seemed less appropriate. On slowing down for closer inspection, however, I saw they had 'parking space at rear for patrons only.' This would provide a good place to disappear for half an hour or so, if such was ever required. By the same token, a lay-by obscured behind a dense row of poplar trees promised to be very handy. My casual research allowed me to build up a composite picture of what a typical trip from Long Reach to Eden Lacy (and back) might be like, given the various needs of an average Scheme employee. It also occurred to me that in timing the run tomorrow I should make allowances for at least some of the layover points I'd spotted.

Drawing nearer to the Ring Road I began seeing UniVans parked at various tried-and-tested locations, as their crews waited for the afternoon to tick away. Sometimes they were gathered together in groups, and five or six men stood holding a discussion on some subject or other. Elsewhere, a pair of feet sticking through a cab window indicated a driver enjoying a tranquil doze. Meanwhile, his assistant sat in the sunshine reading a newspaper. The weather had now turned definitely spring-like, and as I swept along those byways I knew we could look forward to some fine days ahead.

About a mile from Long Reach I saw Chris Peachment strolling along the pavement looking very much at peace with the world. When he saw me he gave a cheery wave, and then mimed as if writing his signature on something. This told me he'd managed to wangle an early swerve, even though it was only half past three in the afternoon!

Five minutes later I arrived in the yard, having noticed a couple of UniVans loitering round a nearby corner. I was first back, and if I'd wanted I could have parked my vehicle on the bay and gone straight home.

For some reason I instead decided to put it through the automatic wash. This stood poised and ready for use at the far end of the yard, so without hesitation I drove in between the giant rollers. The process was well under-way when I saw Bill Harper's UniVan come in through the gateway and head directly towards me. Only when he saw that the wash was occupied did he stop and get out. Then he came over.

'What are you doing?' he asked.

'Washing my van,' I replied.

'But I always wash mine at this time.'

'Sorry,' I shrugged. 'Beat you to it.'

Over in the super's office, Horsefall was stirring be-hind the glass, obviously aware that two vehicles had come back unusually early. Unfortunately, there was only room in the wash for one at a time. If I could I would have moved mine immediately, because all of a sudden I felt quite dog-in-the-mangerish. I never both-ered washing vans as a rule, since they were clean enough anyway, and had only put mine through for the sake of it. Now, however, it was completely engulfed in soapy water, so I had to leave it in for the rinse.

'Thanks very much!' snapped Bill, before stomping back to his van and reversing it fiercely onto the bay.

I watched with alarm as he was confronted by Horsefall. There then followed a lot of arm-waving and finger-jabbing, but as far as I could see Bill didn't get booked. I waited until he'd gone before I put my vehicle on the bay, handed in the keys and went home.

As if getting on the wrong side of Bill wasn't enough,

when I went into the duty room next morning I was instantly called over to the counter by Bob Little. He didn't look very pleased.

'You know that pallet trolley you were supposed to take to Merry Park?'

'Oh yes?'

'How come it's still in the back of UV55?'

'Well,' I said. 'I tried to hand it over, but no one was interested, so I left it in the van.'

'So we've heard.'

'Is that a problem then?'

'Course it's a problem. They've been crying out for that trolley up the Park. I had them on the phone all day yesterday. Then Peter Lawrence tried to deliver it and found there was no docket.'

'That's cos I've got it,' I said. 'As a matter of fact, the docket's in my pocket.'

'This is no laughing matter,' said Bob. 'They've got Scapens coming round inspecting the premises in two days' time.'

'Who's Scapens?'

'Senior Gold Badge. If he sees they've got no manual trolley they'll be in trouble, so they really need it urgent.'

'Here you are then,' I said, unfolding the document in question. 'Give this to Peter and everything'll be alright.'

Bob gave me a prolonged look. 'How long have you been on The Scheme?'

'Five years.'

'Well, then,' he said. 'You know I can't take dockets off people. You'll have to sort it out directly with Peter.'

'Alright then. Sorry about that.'

I left the duty room feeling annoyed that what had promised to be another pleasant day was already marred. Because there'd been no need to clock on, I'd taken my time coming to work, not arriving until a few minutes after eight. This meant I'd missed Peter Lawrence, who was bound to have departed already. I also knew he wouldn't be best pleased at being lumbered with a trolley he couldn't get rid of, so I'd be in his bad books as well as Bill Harper's and Bob Little's. All in all it wasn't a very good start to the morning.

Moreover, I still had to run the gauntlet of Arthur and his blessed key collection. The way he guarded them would make anyone think he was custodian of some sacred artefacts, or maybe even the crown jewels. He passed a remark about how the keys for UV61 had been returned 'inordinately early' the previous afternoon, and only when he could think of no further means to delay me did he hand them over.

Not until I actually got into my cab did yesterday's feeling of liberation return. Ah, yes, there was nothing to beat the freedom of the open road! I checked my time of leaving and headed out through the gates.

I'd decided that the correct way to carry out a timing run would be to stick rigidly to the speed limits for the entire journey. As a result I found myself trundling along deserted sections of road at 30mph when 45 would have been quite safe. Nevertheless, the exercise proved quite enjoyable, and I discovered I could be much more patient than I'd ever thought. At Jimmy's cafe I paused for twenty minutes to allow for 'unscheduled stoppages'. I didn't go in, though, as I was already looking forward to the hospitality at Eden Lacy.

Neither was I to be disappointed. As I came up the concrete drive I again saw Harold, Martin and Eric standing on the loading bay in their silent vigil, watching my approach. Again, too, I was offered tea the moment I arrived.

'Better tell Jim,' said Harold, and once more Martin used the phone on the wall to ring over to the workshop.

'Jim?' he said. 'It's Martin here. We're making a cup of tea if you're interested. Right you are. See you in five minutes.'

After he'd hung up I said, 'Don't mind me asking, but wouldn't it be easier just to shout across to the workshop?'

'You could,' replied Martin. 'But you'd soon be hoarse.'

At twelve o'clock, while I was helping Eric sweep the bay, Keith and Rodney arrived in the Bell Tower van. They were quickly unloaded, and then we all sat round the table for a game of cards.

'Have a good journey back yesterday?' asked Harold, as he shuffled the pack.

'Yes, thanks,' I replied. 'I was in the yard by twenty-five to four.'

'Nice early swerve for you then.'

'It's job-and-finish really,' I said. 'But I suppose it amounts to the same thing.'

'Well, whatever you call it,' said Keith. 'I've got a feeling there'll be a clampdown very soon.'

'How come?'

'I was talking to John Jones this morning. Do you know John?'

'Yes,' I said. 'Keeps the gate at Merry Park.'

'Right, well he told me there's been a big surge in early swerves lately, but it only came to light when Nesbitt signed somebody's card.'

'Nesbitt?' said Martin, clearly astonished.

'Yep,' said Keith. 'Apparently it's the first time he's done it for years, but then he noticed someone else's signature repeated about a dozen times. Turned out to be Gosling—he's a super over at Blackwell depot—and now Nesbitt's conducting this special enquiry. There's bound to be a clampdown when it all comes out.'

Harold nodded and puffed out his cheeks.

'Yes, we've heard of Gosling,' he said. 'Very popular with all the drivers who come here.'

'Well, according to John he's been suspended,' said Keith. 'While the matter's being investigated.'

Under the circumstances I thought it better to keep quiet about my part in Gosling's undoing. All the same, I couldn't help feeling sorry for him.

'Blimey,' I remarked. 'Poor Gosling.'

'Poor all of us,' murmured Keith. 'Imagine life without early swerves!'

On Friday morning I bumped into Jonathan, just after he'd received his first full wage packet. He was standing in the corridor outside the duty room, staring in disbelief at his pay slip.

'Just had a pleasant surprise, have you?' I asked.

'I'll say I have,' he replied. 'Really, I had no idea I'd get paid this much. I was only on the basic rate during training, but look at all these extras: cost of living allowance! Dry-cleaning disbursement! Attendance award! There's even a productivity bonus!'

'Of course.'

'But how can we have a productivity bonus when we don't produce anything?'

'It's a notional payment,' I explained. 'Equivalent to what we might earn in a comparative industry.'

He shook his head and smiled. 'Blimey! Now I see why everyone goes on about glorious days.'

'Ah, but it's not just the money,' I said. 'It's the whole thing. Once you're on The Scheme they look after you right down the line. Just think about it. You've got your full uniform provided, winter and summer, so that saves on clothes; you've got your subsidized catering, your welfare fund, your sports association and your on-site amenities, and all you've got to do is turn up for work every day! It's like being in a great big feather bed! Can I see that?'

'Sure.'

He handed me the pay slip, and I ran my eyes down the itemized list until I found what I was looking for.

'Here you go. Holiday entitlement. You've only been here a week and you've accumulated half a day already. It builds up pro rata.'

'Marvellous,' said Jonathan. 'I think I'll keep this as a souvenir.' He took back the slip and carefully folded it up with his bank notes. Then, as we walked round to the loading bay, he asked a question that surprised me. 'So what exactly's the purpose of all these crates then?'

'You must know,' I said. 'Didn't they tell you during training?'

'No, they just said it was very important.'

'Oh, it's important alright. The whole Scheme depends on it.'

'What is it then?'

'Well, presumably they told you that these UniVans were custom built: specially designed with interchangeable parts and immunity to rust.'

'Yes,' said Jonathan. 'And the engineers can take them to pieces in a day.'

'Right,' I said. 'Well, that's what's in the crates.'

'What, you mean spare parts?'

'No, *all* the parts. Everything. Wheels, panels, mudguards, mirrors, lamps. Not to mention all the engine components. Look at this crate here: what's it say on the label? Radiator grilles: one dozen. There you are: perfect example.'

'So we're driving round in UniVans, full of bits of UniVan?'

'Correct,' I said. 'It's self-perpetuating. We move the parts from one depot to the next, and it keeps us all in work.'

I was quite pleased with my explanation, which I thought had come over as clear and succinct. In thoughtful silence Jonathan gazed at the unhurried activity taking place all along the bay.

'By the way,' he said. 'What's this rumour about no more early swerves?'

'Where've you heard that then?' I asked.

'It's what they're all saying up the canteen.'

'Oh yes?'

'You don't go up there very often do you?'

'No, I prefer a bit of peace and quiet with my dinner.'

'Well, the word is that there's going to be a clamp-down and no one'll get signed off early any more.'

'I'll believe that when I see it,' I said. 'They threaten these purges from time to time to shake everybody up, but then nothing happens. I expect someone thought of this latest one to get the Silver Badges running up and down a bit. At the end of the day it's all just Scheme, isn't it?'

'Suppose so.' Jonathan glanced at his watch. 'Right, I'd better get moving.'

Before he went I gave him the docket for the pallet trolley, and asked him to pass it on to Peter Lawrence.

Then, at last, the wretched thing could be got rid of. After that I went across to the cafe for a tea and dough-nut. I was in no particular hurry to get going, of course, and I now understood why Steve Moore had taken so long over his breakfast the other morning.

Eventually, however, I decided it was time to leave, so I wandered back to the depot and got the keys for UV61. I'd left it parked on the bay overnight, down at the far end near the super's office. As I approached I noticed a slight change in its appearance. Just below the window on the cab door, someone had drawn a sim-ple emblem. It had been done neatly in yellow wax crayon, and consisted of a figure 8 enclosed in a square.

8

'Vandalism,' said a voice nearby. 'Sheer vandalism.'

Glancing round I saw that I'd been joined by Horsefall. He was standing just behind me, gazing thoughtfully at the yellow mark.

'Who's done that then?' I asked.

'You tell me,' he replied. 'The Scheme gets through about half a ton of crayon every year. Anybody can get their hands on it.'

'Must be a flat-day man trying to make a point.'

'Quite possibly, yes, but I don't think it's one person acting on their own. I've heard these signs have been appearing all over the place lately. There've been reports of them from right across the region.'

He produced a handkerchief from his pocket and moved close to the van. Then he began rubbing at the emblem, gradually obliterating it. This was a slow task because the crayon had a high wax content. Eventually, however, all traces of the figure eight were gone.

'That's better,' said Horsefall, stepping back and examining his handiwork.

'I'm surprised you went to all that trouble to get rid of it,' I said. 'I thought you supers would be sympathetic to the flat-dayers.'

'It depends on the situation,' he answered. 'Obviously we favour the full eight hours where it's at all possible, but our main concern is to get the vans back to the depot on time. We don't want you stuck out there in some traffic jam when we're trying to shut the gates for the night, do we?'

'Suppose not.'

'There you are then. In circumstances like that we'd gladly sign your card. We superintendents have homes to go to as well, you know.'

This seemed doubtful, but I let the remark pass and watched as Horsefall returned his now-yellow handkerchief to his pocket.

'So you'd side with the early swervers in some situations, would you?'

'It's not a question of siding with anyone,' he said. 'It's a question of getting the vans back on time.'

I could tell by Horsefall's tone of voice that he was prepared to discuss the matter no further. Nonetheless, I had plenty to think about as I began my drive to Eden Lacy. It appeared there were some people who regarded the flat day in very serious terms. I knew already that men like Len Walker and John Ford were outspoken practitioners, and indeed they'd been spreading the word against early swerves for as long as I could remember. Somehow, however, I couldn't imagine either of them going around daubing emblems all over the place. Not long after I'd got onto the Ring Road, I spotted just such a device drawn on the back of a UniVan travelling ahead of me. It was identical to the one on my cab door, and had again been done in yellow wax crayon. I tried to overtake the van to catch a glimpse of its driver, but at the exact moment I drew level he turned up a side-street and I lost sight of him. A little while later I met a UniVan approaching in the opposite direction. By now I'd run into a spot of slow-moving traffic, so that I was barely doing more than 5mph when I drew alongside the oncoming vehicle. This had plates bearing the letters TL, which indicated it came from a different region. And there, just below the cab window, was yet another enclosed figure eight. I glanced at the yellow emblem, then up at the driver, only to realize that both he and his assistant were looking across at me. When they caught my gaze they each gave me a thumbs-up signal, as if reaffirming some common bond. I nodded and smiled vaguely, they smiled in return, and next instant we'd passed by.

Now as I mentioned before, drivers on The Scheme only acknowledged one another when they belonged to the same depot, and they always did so by flashing their lights. This thumbs-up signal was not a recognized form of greeting and therefore meant nothing. All the same, I got the strong impression that the occupants of the other van had been trying to communicate with me, and that they were offering more than just a simple hello. Rather, they seemed to be counting me as one of their number. The evidence suggested that certain parties had organized themselves into some kind of movement, with its own special emblem, and were now conducting a recruitment drive in order to strengthen their cause. How successful the campaign would be was impossible to tell, but I now had no doubt that the flat-dayers were on the march!

Speculation was rife when I turned up at Eden Lacy that morning. Despite being stuck out in their remote corner of The Scheme, miles from anywhere, Harold and his companions had heard all sorts of reports and rumours since my last visit, and were eager to pass them on. Over platefuls of Martin's sandwiches, I was told of impromptu meetings where the flat-dayers had begun to speak up and make themselves known to one another. Such gatherings had taken place more or less spontaneously at various depots across the country, and it had soon emerged that, far from being the tiny minority everyone always assumed, these men actually represented a sizeable body, amounting to roughly half the total workforce. Soon afterwards they'd adopted the enclosed figure eight as their popular emblem, and thereby earned the scorn of the early swerve brigade.

Even so, these stories were only the tip of the iceberg. When Keith and Rodney arrived just after midday, they brought news of a further development. It seemed that some of the more extreme flat-dayers had stopped taking their ten-off-the-eight, and were now refusing to even contemplate clocking off work until four thirty at the earliest. Moreover, the previous day had been the first in living memory when no one in the entire Scheme had had their card signed before the end of their duty. This pearl of information was saved until last, and Keith seemed to take some pleasure from the uneasy stir that passed around the table as its meaning sunk in.

'But I thought you were an early swerver,' I remarked.

'Oh, I am,' said Keith. 'Without a doubt.'

'So how come you look so pleased then?'

'Because there are still some who don't realize the seriousness of the threat. Perhaps this'll shake them up a bit.'

Harold sighed. 'Do you know we've only had one early swerve at this depot in all the time we've been here? That was when Nesbitt turned up on Christmas Eve and said we could go home at half past three.'

'Nice of him.'

'But all the rest of the year we're de facto flat-dayers.'

'Speak for yourself!' snapped Martin. 'I haven't made up my mind which side I'm on yet.'

In the past week I'd decided for definite that Harold and Martin must be father and son. Not only were their appearances similar, but they often tended to bicker in the way people do when they spend a lot of time together. It was common at Eden Lacy to hear Martin's high-pitched voice raised in objection to some comment made by Harold. These squabbles weren't usually over points of high principle, however, and more often referred to petty matters such as how many spoonfuls of tea should go in the pot. I was surprised, therefore, that Martin had taken exception to being labelled a 'de facto flat-dayer'. It was unlike him to be concerned with anything so esoteric. On the other hand, there was no escaping the fact that an important issue was at stake, as Keith had so rightly pointed out. For every man who believed firmly in working the full eight hour day, it seemed there was another whose sole intention was to get his card signed and go home early. Furthermore, the two sides were finding it increasingly difficult to see eye to eye. At the moment, this tiny depot lay on the periphery of the debate, with few outside influences. Things were likely to change, though, when the new schedules were introduced. After that the number of crews arriving each day would multiply greatly, and they were bound to bring their opinions with them.

On my return trip that afternoon I found myself closely scrutinizing every UniVan I passed, to see if any bore the flat-dayers' emblem. I counted five that did even before I got back to the Ring Road, and these included two vehicles from our own circuit. What also caught my attention were the groups of drivers I saw standing by their vans in the various lay-bys and pull-ins along the way. Previously I'd supposed these gatherings to consist of friends and acquaintances discussing external matters such as sport or the weather. Now, though, I began to wonder if they weren't drawn together by a common cause. For it struck me that if the flat-dayers had started to associate more closely, then the early swervers would have no choice other than to follow suit.

I peered at the assorted groups and tried to work out which side they were on. Oh yes, it was true that all these men looked the same in their blue shirts, but I knew for a fact they were divided into two distinct types.

The flat-dayers had the advantage, of course, because they already had a campaign underway. This point was confirmed when I passed beneath the railway bridge at Fiveways Junction. The bridge had a vast steel span that had been plastered with slogans and symbols for as long as I could remember. Most comprised odd words such as ZILCH and BANOPS, whose meanings were known only to those who wielded the paintbrush. There was also a depiction of a smiling, noseless face, and a splodge that roughly resembled a camel. It must have taken a feat of daring for anybody to get up there, but, to tell the truth, I'd seen these daubings so many times I hardly took any notice of them. Today, however, I spotted a new addition to the motley collection, namely, a gigantic figure eight set inside a square. Someone certainly meant business. This being a Friday, I thought it might be an idea to beat the traffic and get back to Long Reach in good time, so I put my foot down and rolled into the yard around three o'clock. The place was quiet, with the afternoon rush yet to begin. Given all the rumours I'd heard during the day, it would have been interesting to observe the other UniVans as they returned, to see who'd got an early swerve, for example, or to identify any noticeable differences in the way the flat-dayers clocked off. Trouble was, it involved hanging round for at least half an hour, so in the end I decided that further behavioural studies could wait. Instead, I parked the van opposite the loading bay, handed in the keys, and went home.

On Monday morning my interest in the subject had to be set aside once more. George was back from his fortnight's holiday, and he quickly reminded me that his concerns lay elsewhere.

'Trace is going to skin you alive,' he announced, when I met him outside the duty room.

'That's a relief,' I said. 'I was expecting much worse than that.'

We shook hands.

'How was your break?'

'Terrible,' said George. 'She had me running round like a headless chicken, trying to get those cakes sorted out. What happened to our arrangement?'

I told him about the timing runs and my daily trips to Eden Lacy.

'And how long's it going to go on for?' he asked.

'There's a few more days to do yet.'

'That explains why I've been stood down.'

'Oh well,' I said. 'Looks like you're in for a nice easy time.'

'I don't want a nice easy time!' he protested. 'I want

to be out on the road! I've got a huge backlog of orders to work through! I've got cakes waiting to be collected from Sandro. I've got Ken Scanlon on my back about all those boxes in the workshop, and on top of all that I've got Trace complaining night and day.'

'Sounds like a bit of a headache.'

'It is, mate,' he said. 'I assure you it is.'

As consolation I took him over to the cafe for a cup of tea and a doughnut. Then, to take his mind off the problem of the cakes, I told him what had been happening while he was away. When he heard about the flat-dayers' activities he remarked that he'd noticed no difference during his time off.

'The Scheme looks just the same from the outside,' he said. 'UniVans driving round and round in the mornings, and parked all over the place in the afternoons. Nothing new there.'

'But these are serious developments,' I insisted.

'Yah,' said George. 'You're probably just imagining it.'

A little later he went up to the games room to mope and fret about his cakes, while I headed off for yet another run to Eden Lacy. By now I had a good 'feel' of how long the journey would take in each direction, along with a comprehensive list of times, and, to tell the truth, further trips were completely unnecessary. Nevertheless, Ray Coppin had suggested I did the timing runs for ten days, so ten days I would do. I was in no particular hurry to return to normal duties, and decided to make the most of my privileged status while I still had the chance.

Someone else just back from his holidays was Richard Harper. I passed him and Bill on the Ring Road at about half past ten, and guessed they must be on a return journey from Rudgeway. The familiar sight of the two brothers working together reminded me of the recent incident at the vehicle wash when I'd inadvertently crossed Bill. I still hadn't cleared that up with him, and it then occurred to me that I had hardly spoken to anyone from our own depot in over a week. Except for the odd brief conversation I'd remained aloof from the day-to-day affairs of Long Reach, preferring grandly to speculate about The Scheme in general. All of a sudden I realized I'd become cut off from my colleagues. As the Harper brothers' UniVan went past I flashed my lights in greeting, but there was no response. This was disquieting because Bill was a friend who went back a long way. He'd been the first person to speak to me when I started at the depot, and I didn't want to fall out with him over a minor episode. I decided, therefore, that the situation would have to be put right at the first possible opportunity.

Having said that, I had to admit I was enjoying my role as roving envoy. It was a pleasure having a UniVan to myself, and especially so with UV61. The vehicle offered one of the most comfortable drives in the fleet, and as the road unrolled beneath its wheels I began to toy with the idea of taking a more circumlocutory route this morning. Maybe, I thought, I could go to Eden Lacy via Castle Gate, just for a change. With this in mind I left the Ring Road earlier than usual and headed north along New River Way. According to my regional map, this would take me onto the Northern Loop, which passed fairly close to the Gate. It was some while since I'd been up this road, but I was sure it would be all quite straightforward once I'd recognized a couple of landmarks. My optimistic plan started to go wrong, however, when I saw a red-and-white sign that said DIVERTED TRAFFIC BEAR LEFT. As I was unaware of having been diverted, I decided this didn't apply to me and continued going dead ahead. After another couple of miles I came to an unmarked T-junction. Here I turned left, assuming that I was now on the Loop, and that even if I wasn't, I was bound to meet up with it eventually. My assumption proved wrong on both counts. The road I'd chosen turned out to be nothing more than a link between a series of roundabouts, whose only purpose, apparently, was to hinder my progress. I could find no trace of these roundabouts on the part of the map where I thought I was, so I stopped using it and continued to follow my nose instead. Only when I saw a sign directing me back to the Ring Road did I accept that I'd gone the wrong way. This in itself would have been tolerable, though rather irritating, if the van hadn't then begun to lose power. I'd already noticed once or twice during the journey that it wasn't going with its usual vigour, and now, as the engine failed, I realized why: I was out of diesel.

Now I should say immediately that it wasn't my job to put fuel in UniVans. This was The Scheme for Full

Employment, don't forget, and such tasks were supposed to be taken care of nightly by the shift engineers. As a matter of fact, I'd been aware that the fuel gauge had indicated empty from the moment I'd taken the van out, but since it had said the same thing for the whole of the previous week I'd supposed it to be faulty and ignored it. Today, however, it didn't just say empty: it said very empty. With a dying moan the engine fell silent and I came to a halt at the roadside.

I got out and looked round at the place I'd inadvertently chosen to stop. Brilliant! Not a cafe in sight! No newsagent! No library! Not even a nearby park with a convenient bench and a duck pond! In short, nowhere to pass the time while I waited to be rescued. I was surrounded by industrial units, all set back from the road behind ugly security fences. With a sigh I began searching for a phone box. This took some doing, but eventually I found one, then fumbled in my inside pocket for the engineers' emergency number. A few seconds later I was speaking to Rob Marshall. When he heard I was out of fuel, he sighed too.

'Where are you exactly?'

'In a phone box,' I replied. 'Friendship Drive, it says here.'

'Never heard of it.'

'No, nor me. I think I'm quite near the Ring Road, though. Haven't you got a map in that office of yours?'

'Course we have,' he said. 'Alright. Stay with the van and we'll come and look for you.'

I wandered back, knowing that I wouldn't see Rob for at least two hours. Engineers couldn't just drop what they were doing and come out in search of stranded vehicles, so I resigned myself to sitting in the cab in the middle of nowhere, and waiting. Really I should have known I was on the wrong road by the lack of UniVans swanning past. I hadn't laid eyes on one for some while now, a sure sign that I'd run into some backwater. In one way, however, this was a blessing in disguise, because if I'd broken down on a busy thoroughfare I'd have had to put up with the taunts of passing drivers for running out of diesel.

I settled down in the dummy seat with my feet up on the dashboard, trying to get as comfortable as possible. Then I glanced around the van's spartan interior, at the huge steering wheel, the handbrake, and the set of simple controls, whose configuration was so familiar to me.

Stencilled in black, just above the windscreen, were the vehicle details:

HEIGHT:	10' 2"
WIDTH:	8' 0"
LENGTH:	19' 6"

I gazed at these figures as I'd gazed at them many times before. I gazed through the windscreen at the factory units, looking for signs of life. And I gazed into the wing mirror. To my surprise there was a man standing there. For a moment I thought Rob Marshall had somehow managed to arrive in complete silence, but dismissed the idea the instant I saw the newcomer's clothes. Instead of blue engineers' overalls he was dressed in a faded suit that appeared to be one size too small for him. He also carried a sort of shopping bag with long handles, and when he put this down and produced a notebook and pencil, I knew at once that I'd been targeted by an enthusiast. Where he'd appeared from I had no idea, since I'd noticed no other pedestrians when I walked to the phone box. Perhaps, I thought, he belonged to one of the buildings nearby. Hoping he'd think I was asleep I remained sitting very still, watching through half-closed eyes as he began an inspection of the vehicle. Fortunately, these enthusiasts were far more interested in UniVans than the people who actually drove them, so I thought it unlikely that he would bother me. Indeed, he marched round as if he owned the thing, jotting down various observations in his book before getting out a camera to take a photograph. From the silence of my cab I watched as this preoccupied man scurried round pursuing his hobby, and wondered, not for the first time, how anyone could devote their whole life to the study of UniVans! At one stage he looked directly at me. Unable to avert my gaze quickly enough, I decided the best thing was to acknowledge him with a casual nod. In return I received a ghastly grin, which confirmed my long-held belief that all the enthusiasts were barmy.

Finally he wandered off, presumably in search of yet another UniVan to record in his notebook, while I eased back for a quiet doze. Couldn't complain really, being paid to sleep, and I had to admit the dummy seat was quite comfy. I slumbered for well over an hour, before being woken by the double beep of a horn. Rob had arrived in the service van.

Blearily I got out to say hello, expecting him to berate me for not reporting that the fuel was low. Instead, however, he began making excuses for the engineers, saying they were run off their feet dealing with UniVans on normal duties, and that my vehicle wasn't actually scheduled to be on the road this week. Having thus avoided the question of blame, we shared a few derogatory remarks about 'the management,' and then Rob opened the back doors of his van. Inside were several cans containing enough diesel to get me through the rest of the day. I watched as he replenished my tank, and a few minutes later I was ready to go. Inevitably, there was a docket to sign, which Rob described as unimportant but necessary, and at last I could continue my journey. Very carefully I checked my map to make sure I didn't go the wrong way again, then I said cheerio to Rob and set off.

When eventually I arrived at Eden Lacy, it was twenty to three in the afternoon. I'd usually departed by this time, but I had no reason to expect anything to be different from the easy-going atmosphere of the mornings. I was a little disconcerted, therefore, when Harold and the others virtually ignored me. Apart from a brief glance in my direction as I pulled into the yard, their attention seemed mainly to be on a UniVan already parked on the bay. This was identified by the letters CT, and while the three of them busied themselves getting several pallets loaded, its crew stood some distance away, watching in silence. As I came up the steps there was none of the friendly banter going on that I normally associated with Eden Lacy: no playing cards or promising mugs of tea lay on the table, nor was there any sign of Jim, who generally wandered over from his workshop on the slightest pretext. Even so, I went and joined the driver and his assistant in an attempt to establish some kind of rapport. As I approached they gazed at me, but offered no form of greeting.

'Alright?' I said.

'Alright,' one of them replied.

The other turned away slightly, and seemed to be watching Harold as he fussed around with a pallet trolley. This in itself was a rare sight. Normally, Eric took charge of loading operations while Harold kept his hands firmly in his pocket. Today, though, things were being done differently.

'Nice depot this, isn't it?' I ventured.

The man who'd been watching Harold now turned and regarded me with incredulity.

'Nice?'

'Yes.'

'What are you talking about? It's useless here.'

'But it's really friendly.'

He shook his head. 'How long have you been on The Scheme?'

'About five years.'

'Well, you must be mad then.'

'Why?'

'Cos you can't get a swerve here, can you?!' he snapped. 'There's no supers to sign your card!'

'No, but . . .'

'There's no buts about it,' said his companion. 'This is the most useless depot in the region.'

I didn't really like the way this conversation was going, yet I could hardly just walk away from the pair, so I changed the subject instead.

'I've been driving out here daily from Long Reach,' I said. 'Been doing some timing runs.'

'What for?'

'Our circuit's being extended. There's going to be new schedules and everything, so we'll be coming here regularly.'

At this the two men laughed out loud. 'Well,' said one of them. 'Lucky you.'

By now Harold and his team had finished loading the UniVan and begun sweeping the bay at the far end. Their action caused me to glance at my watch, and I suddenly realized it was gone three o'clock!

'Right,' I announced. 'Better go. Nice talking to you.'

'Yeah,' they murmured.

I gave a wave to the others as I descended the steps, but they didn't seem to notice, so I got back into my cab and departed.

The circumstances of my trip to Eden Lacy had left me with an odd feeling of disquiet. Suddenly I wondered if I'd become isolated from the mainsteam of opinion in The Scheme. Certainly I'd been taken aback by the remarks of the crew from CT depot, wherever that was. Judging by the way they spoke, anyone would have assumed that the early swervers were a churlish bunch, interested in nothing but getting their cards signed. Yet when I thought of Keith and Rodney, who were both avowed swervers, I realized you couldn't label a whole group by the behaviour of a minority. Those two liked nothing better than a trip to Eden Lacy, and only began to think of early swerves as their day drew to a close. All the same, it was becoming clear that attitudes were hardening, and I realized I'd been blissfully unaware of the situation. All this I considered on my journey back to Long Reach. Traffic had built up, and by the time I arrived it was almost a quarter to five. There was no one around except Collis, who stood inside the gates waiting to lock up. (The gatekeepers themselves finished work at four thirty.)

'Haven't you got a home to go to?' he asked, as I drove slowly past him. I didn't bother to answer.

All this set the tone for my remaining few days on the timing runs. When I returned to Eden Lacy next morning everything had gone back to normal, and I enjoyed a nice game of cards round the table with the others. Nevertheless, I was conscious that the novelty of these journeys was beginning to wear off. On the way out I'd passed the Harper brothers on the Ring Road, only for my flashed greeting to be ignored once more. I really needed to be back on my normal duties so I could have a proper talk with Bill. As if to emphasize this point, travelling home the same afternoon I saw UV55, my usual vehicle, being driven by George, with Jonathan in the dummy seat! How George had wangled this I had no idea, but I knew his intentions alright. Our rostered duty included a trip between Blackwell and Rudgeway depots, which meant going straight past Sandro's Bakery. George had evidently grown impatient with being stood down, and persuaded someone to let him take over the duty on a temporary basis. As an assistant driver he was qualified to do this (just about), but a few rules must have been bent to allow it actually to happen. Seeing him behind the wheel of our UniVan only added to my sense of detachment.

Those last few trips went by pleasantly enough, however, and it didn't seem long before I was back in Ray Coppin's office with my list of timings.

'Get on alright, did you?' he asked, as he sat scanning the figures.

'Yes, thanks.'

'That's good.' He opened a drawer and placed the list inside. 'I'll have to get these off to Merry Park sometime, when I've got a minute.'

'Any idea when the new schedules will start?' I enquired.

'Ooh, not for a while yet,' he replied. 'It's all got to be reviewed first.'

'Er . . . oh.'

'Can't see any changes for the time being.'

Next morning I resumed my normal duty, clocking on at ten to eight. I think George was a bit disappointed to be relinquishing command of our vehicle, but he returned to the dummy seat without much complaint. The run was triangular, calling at Merry Park, Blackwell and Rudgeway, and hence ideal for George's purposes. He'd managed to clear his backlog of cakes over the past few days, but there were always new ones to deal with. Today we had four boxes to drop off at Sandro's. Arriving at Blackwell around dinner time, I was alarmed to discover that Gosling was still under suspension. I didn't bother asking Osgood what would become of him because supers were never forthcoming on such matters, but amongst the depot staff all manner of speculation was offered. Charlie Green, for example, told me that 'Mr' Gosling was being greatly missed, and that the management would be 'mistaken' not to reinstate him at the earliest opportunity. Mick Dalston agreed with this to an extent, but pointed out that Gosling wasn't the only super who'd signed people's cards with such generosity.

'Surely there'll be others to take his place,' he conjectured.

'Maybe so,' said Charlie. 'But there'll never be another like him.'

Len Walker, meanwhile, talked in high moral tones about 'just deserts' coming to the early swervers and their benefactors. It was Len, of course, who'd been first to voice concern about the way standards were slipping on The Scheme, and he now seemed to be regarded as a kind of sage, especially by the flat-dayers. George told me how, on one occasion during my absence, Len had sat on his forklift truck holding forth about the sanctity of the eight-hour day, while a small group of drivers and their assistants listened closely.

'If you ask me,' commented George, 'those flat-dayers are too self-righteous. They seem to think they're the only ones who do any work.'

'Well, they are, aren't they?' I said.

'Not really,' he replied. 'They might think they are, but in truth, the early swervers just manage their time better.'

'Does that make you a swerver then?'

'I'm not anything,' George announced. 'I'm only interested in delivering my cakes.'

With this in mind we headed off for Rudgeway, calling at Sandro's place en route. George went in with the usual stack of boxes, and when he emerged I thought he had a rather sheepish look about him.

'What is it?' I asked.

'Nothing really,' he said. 'Except that I could really do with getting back to Long Reach by four o'clock. There's a kiddies' party, you see.' By way of explanation, he showed me the single cake box he'd just collected.

'But you didn't bother mentioning it till now.'

'No,' said George. 'I mean yes. Correct.'

'Well, I suppose we could try and get a swerve from Rudgeway,' I suggested. 'And leave there a bit sharp.'

He sighed. 'Trouble is, I've already made tentative enquiries in that quarter. The supers are getting quite cagey about signing anything after what happened to Gosling.'

'What do you propose then?'

'Can't we just go early and risk it?'

'You're joking.'

'Oh, come on,' pleaded George. 'Just this once.'

I considered his desperate request. Needless to say, there was no such thing as 'just this once' where George was concerned, but I thought I could see a solution to the current problem.

'Tell you what,' I said. 'Horsefall's seen me returning early for the past ten days. He probably won't even notice if we slip in quietly.'

'What about Collis?'

'He shouldn't be a problem.'

So it was agreed we would risk it. Once again, I thought, I'd gone out of my way to accommodate George, or more accurately his girlfriend, and all I'd get out of the arrangement would be a returned favour at some unspecified future date. Still, that was the way things were on The Scheme, so I cooperated. As it happened, we hadn't been to Rudgeway depot for quite some while prior to starting this duty, so we weren't very well known there. Consequently, it seemed OK to leave as soon as we'd been loaded, some fifteen minutes ahead of schedule. By the time we got to Long Reach I'd gained another five simply by putting my foot down.

I stopped outside the gates. 'Go on then,' I said. 'Off you go.'

'No, it's alright,' George replied. 'I'll come in with you. I need to see Ken Scanlon for a sec.'

'Suit yourself.'

I pulled into the yard as casually as I could, hoping no one would notice. For a moment this seemed highly likely, since there was no sign of Horsefall, Gosling, or any of the other usual supers. Our hopes faded, however, when we were confronted by an individual in a black peaked cap, black jacket and medium-length black skirt.

'Blimey,' said George. 'It's a woman.'

9

There was no avoiding her attentions. We were the only vehicle in the yard, and the instant we appeared she glanced at her wristwatch. Then she observed us with a cool expression while I reversed onto the bay. I applied the handbrake and sat behind the wheel as she strode purposefully in our direction. To tell the truth, her unexpected presence had caught me by surprise, and I think the same went for George. Obviously, we were used to seeing women on The Scheme because many were employed in the canteens and offices. We'd even heard that some depots had recently taken a few on as drivers and assistant drivers. Never before, though, had we seen a woman wearing the uniform of a superintendent, and I knew at once that the situation would require extra care.

'Leave this to me,' I murmured. 'I'll handle it.'

Opening the door, I got out of the cab to meet her. She'd stopped about six feet away from the van, and was perusing her schedules book. Then she glanced up.

'Afternoon,' I said, giving her my best smile. 'Welcome to Long Reach.'

'Thank you,' she replied. 'Can I see your duty card please?'

'Er . . . oh, yes. Here you are.'

I handed the card over and she stood peering at it in a knowledgeable manner. From the corner of my eye I noticed George get out of the cab, and begin walking towards the workshop. Wedged under his arm was the cake box.

'Haven't seen you in these quarters before,' I said, adopting a conversational tone.

'No, you won't have,' replied the super. 'I've been transferred from Royal Pond depot.'

'That temporary, is it?'

'Permanent.'

'Oh.'

Now she looked across at George, her eyes focusing directly on the box.

'Spare parts,' he announced, by way of explanation, and continued walking. He'd covered about a third of the distance to the workshop when she spoke again, in a voice clear and terse.

'Stop.'

George stopped.

'Come back.'

He traipsed back and stood before her.

'What sort of spare parts?'

'Well,' said George. 'It's a mixture.'

'Really?' she said. 'Let's have a look then.'

With the colour draining from his face, he prepared to remove the lid.

'That for me?!' called a voice from the workshop door. It was Ken Scanlon.

'Could be!' George called back.

'Bring it over then! I haven't got all day!'

The super gave George a suspicious glance as he shrugged and resumed his journey across the yard. Her gaze was then transferred to Ken, who quickly slipped inside the doorway, after which it settled on me.

I smiled again. 'Expect you meet a lot of interesting people in your line of work, don't you?'

'Not so far, no,' she replied. 'But I suppose there's always a chance.'

In the awkward silence that followed, she again examined our duty card.

'How long have you been on The Scheme?' she asked at length.

'About five years.'

'Well,' she said, handing me the card. 'You should know not to come back early without getting a signature.'

And to my astonishment she took the matter no further.

The time had now ticked round to four fifteen, and one or two vans were beginning to make tentative approaches through the gate. With another glance at her watch, the new superintendent gave me a curt nod, and then began checking off the returning vehicles. At the far end of the workshop I saw George emerge from a different door, still carrying his cake box, and make a hurried escape. A third UniVan rumbled into the yard, and headed straight for the automatic wash. It was being driven by Bill Harper, with Richard sitting beside him in the dummy seat.

Here was my chance to make peace with Bill, so after locking up and getting rid of the keys I wandered over to see him. He was now parked inside the wash mechanism, but for some reason neither he nor Richard had got out of their cab. Instead, they remained seated inside, and as I drew nearer I saw that they were involved in a heated discussion about something. I stopped in my tracks and watched as they gesticulated at one another, their voices raised in a muffled hubbub. Then all of a sudden Bill threw open his door, jumped out, and slammed it behind him. As he marched off towards the loading bay I called his name, but he totally ignored me.

'Bill!' I tried again. 'Bill!'

But it was no good. Next thing he'd gone up the steps and disappeared into the depot's interior, leaving me wondering what the argument could have been about. This entire scene had been witnessed by Ron Curtain, newly-arrived, whose vehicle was next in line for the wash. When he saw my bewildered look he got out and came over.

'Don't think Bill's talking to me,' I remarked.

'He's not talking to anybody,' said Ron. 'Just spends all his time quarrelling with Richard.'

'What about?'

'Well, let's say they have ideological differences.'

We watched as Richard got out of the cab, switched on the machinery, and then stood back as the great rollers began to turn. Seconds later the UniVan was engulfed in foamy water.

'Differences?' I repeated. 'Surely they're both flat-dayers.'

'Course they are,' Ron answered. 'But Bill insists on claiming his ten-off-the-eight so he can get in the wash, whereas Richard wants to forgo it. They've been squabbling for days.'

'Have they?'

'Like a couple of old hens. You'd know that if you came up the canteen a bit more often, instead of spending every dinner time with your van.'

'Who does?'

'You do.'

'Well, only because it's so noisy up there,' I protested. 'You can't hear yourself think sometimes!'

Ron shook his head. 'You don't have to make excuses to me. All I'm saying is there's some momentous debates going on and you're missing out on them all.'

'Oh, right,' I said. 'I didn't realize.'

'Maybe it's time you got a bit more involved.'

'Yeah . . . maybe.'

As the minutes passed by, more and more UniVans were coming into the yard to park up for the evening.

Soon we were joined by Bryan Tovey, whose usually jovial manner had been replaced by a look of acute disgruntlement.

'Yet another swerveless day,' he sighed.

'Well don't come here for sympathy,' Ron answered.

This rather abrupt outburst surprised me, but I was equally taken aback when Bryan snapped, 'Don't worry, mate, I won't!', before turning and walking away.

'Good grief,' I said, after he'd gone. 'That was a bit harsh, wasn't it?'

'Not really, no,' said Ron. 'To tell you the truth I've had it up to my neck with the swervers.'

Jangling his keys he stepped over to his UniVan to lock up. Which was when I noticed something drawn on the door in yellow crayon: a figure eight enclosed in a square.

'But I thought you of all people would be neutral.'

'Neutral's not an option,' he replied. 'These days you're either a flat-dayer or a swerver. There's nothing else.'

The new superintendent's name, apparently, was Joyce. I got this information the following morning from Collis, who'd seen me talking to her from his office window. He joined me on the bay while the van was being loaded, and gave me the benefit of his opinion.

'One to watch, she is,' he announced. 'Very ambitious.'

'Thought she might be.'

'Book you soon as look at you.'

'Well, she seemed alright last night,' I said. 'Firm but fair, sort of thing.'

'Oh, she's always gentle the first time,' said Collis. 'While she's still getting your measure.'

At this moment Joyce came into view at the far end of the bay, having emerged from between two stacks of crates. Her sudden appearance caused Collis instantly to flip open his schedules book and begin leafing through its pages. Then he looked at his watch.

'Come on,' he ordered, in an authoritarian tone. 'It's time you were loaded and away.'

'Alright, alright!' I answered. 'It's all in hand. George has taken charge of loading this morning.'

'That's OK then,' he said, lowering his voice. 'But look lively or you'll have her on your tail.'

And with that he retreated to the sanctuary of his office, forgetting, no doubt, that she was free to join him there if she so wished. At present, though, she seemed content overseeing the general activity on the loading bay. She strolled casually from van to van, nodding at warehousemen and drivers as they bent to their work. George, I noticed, was making a great show of helping Chris Peachment move some particularly large crates onto our vehicle. (They were large because our cargo today consisted of UniVan side panels.) Joyce paused for a while to watch them get the forklift into position, then glanced thoughtfully around the depot's interior. She had a proprietorial air about her, and appeared to be estimating the cubic capacity of the building.

'Isn't it marvellous?' I said, walking over. 'How much can be squeezed under one roof.'

'Well, there doesn't seem to be much squeezing going on here,' she replied. 'It's half empty most of the week.'

'Yes, but it's handy having all that spare room to play with.'

'Handy's not the word I'd have used. Wasteful more like. I'm sure this space could serve a much better purpose.'

'Do you mean ergonomically?'

'No,' said Joyce. 'I mean usefully.'

Unable to grasp the exact gist of what she was saying, I decided the best solution was to change the subject.

'I'm just going over to get some teas before we leave. Can I buy you one?'

'No thanks,' she said. 'I don't drink tea. Or coffee.'

'How do you pass the time then?'

'Quite easily really. For example, I check to see if people are wearing the correct uniform.'

'Ah.'

'Didn't you receive a new issue of shirts this year?'

'Yes, but I prefer the old ones. They're more comfortable.'

'Comfortable doesn't come into it,' said Joyce. 'You get given new ones annually to give the Drapery Department something to do. I'd have thought a man of your intellect would know that.'

Whether this last remark was intended as a compliment or an insult I couldn't tell. Fortunately, I was spared the rigours of further conversation by a loud slamming noise as George closed the roller door. This was the signal that we were ready to leave, so after promising Joyce I would indeed wear a new shirt tomorrow, I went over the road, got the teas, and then joined my assistant on the bay.

'I saw you,' he said. 'Do you fancy her, or something?'

'Course not,' I replied. 'We were just talking, that's all. As a matter of fact she's got some very interesting points of view.'

'Well, don't forget she's still a super at the end of the day.'

'No,' I assured him. 'I won't forget that.'

We watched as Joyce strode towards the office in sensible, black shoes. Then we climbed into the van and headed first to Merry Park, then on to Blackwell, and finally Rudgeway. As I said before, this was a depot we hadn't visited regularly for quite some while, simply because of the way the duty rota was worked out. The only person we knew at all well there was a warehouseman called Reg Pippett, a committed early swerver if ever there was one. As the crates were being unloaded from our van, Reg mentioned the recent dearth of signatures.

'Whatever happened to our precious swerves?' he asked. 'They've vanished without trace.'

'Yes,' I agreed. 'They appear to have gone right out of fashion.'

'Well, I hope they come back in again,' he said, with a grin. 'They were the only thing that kept me going.'

It was quite refreshing talking to Reg, who displayed none of the gloom and doom that I'd come across just lately. Instead, he seemed to accept that the clamp-down was an unavoidable reality, worth little more than a resigned shrug. When I asked him what he thought of the flat-dayers he told me he regarded them as a joke, rather than a threat. True, he said, they were overweening and sanctimonious, but they were also completely harmless, and he was sure the glorious times would return very soon. At four o'clock George and I resumed our journey with Reg's positive words still ringing in our ears. Their resonance was lost, though, when we passed beneath the railway bridge at Fiveways Junction.

'Look at that,' said George, peering upwards.

For a moment I thought he'd only just noticed the gigantic figure eight that I'd spotted the week before. However, when I looked up I saw it had been completely painted over. Now, in its place, was a huge letter g with a long extended tail.

'Where've we seen that before?'

'It's Gosling's signature,' I said. 'The swervers must have adopted it for their campaign.'

'They can't be serious.'

'Oh, I think they are. Very serious indeed.'

Clearly, Reg Pippett's moderate stance wasn't shared by some of his associates, but I had to admit that who-ever had climbed up there had made an excellent job. The stylized letter g was an exact copy of the signature we all knew so well. Also, it was much more flamboyant than the flat-dayers' bland figure eight, which appeared rather puritanical by comparison. And, of course, once we'd become aware of the new device we began seeing it everywhere, most notably on the sides of UniVans. By the end of the duty we'd counted more than half a dozen examples, all done in the same ubiquitous yellow crayon.

Over the next few days the rival insignias became such a common sight that our own vehicle began to be conspicuous for its lack of decoration. We weren't completely alone, as there were still a few other unmarked vans around, but each time we journeyed along the Ring Road I was aware of being part of a shrinking minority. I assumed this was the reason John Jones gave us a prolonged look as we passed beneath his gatehouse at Merry Park one morning. I gave him a cheery wave, for which I received no response, and then headed into the yard. A minute later we were parked on the bay, waiting for someone to come and unload us. We expected the usual delay, but to our surprise Billy Barker surfaced almost immediately, fully equipped with a forklift truck. He got the day's shipment taken off very quickly (for him), before giving us some 'important news'.

'We're holding a mass meeting tomorrow dinner time,' he announced. 'In the light of the present difficulties.'

'Are we invited?' enquired George.

'Certainly you are,' said Billy. 'It should be quite a good turnout. We've invited Les Prentice to address the gathering.'

The way he uttered the name 'Les Prentice' suggested that I was supposed to have heard of him, which I hadn't. There was no doubt, however, that Billy was a swerver, and so I assumed the guest speaker was also from that fraternity.

'OK,' I promised. 'We'll be there.'

'Glad to hear it,' he said. 'We need a few stalwarts in the ranks.'

'Here's Dawson,' said George, with a glance towards the office.

'Right,' said Billy. 'See you tomorrow.'

Quickly he turned on his heels and left us. Next thing we'd been joined by Dawson, who had a completely different agenda on his mind.

'Glad I've caught you,' he said. 'You brought a pallet trolley here the other week, didn't you?'

'Well, not me personally,' I replied. 'It was someone covering my duty.'

'That's good enough for me. Can you take it back again?'

'But I thought you were crying out for a manual trolley.'

'Yes, we were.'

'So what's wrong with it then?'

'Nothing,' Dawson sighed. 'We only wanted it because we'd heard Scapens was coming to inspect the premises. You know of him, do you?'

'Yeah,' I said. 'Senior Gold Badge, isn't he?'

'Correct. Top of the league, and a very dogged customer.'

'What, worse than Nesbitt?'

'Oh yes, much worse. And when we realized we hadn't got a trolley there was total panic. A big call went out to all the depots for a spare one, but it wasn't co-ordinated properly.'

'What happened then?'

'We got too many, didn't we? When Scapens carried out his inspection he found three manual trolleys scattered about the place. Then he put in a report saying the equipment wasn't distributed evenly, and the upshot is you've got to take it back.'

'Where?'

'Anywhere,' said Dawson. 'As long as it's out of here.'

He broke off, marched over to the corner, and returned pushing a pallet trolley. The one with the bent handle. We put it in the rear of the van and secured it to the bulkhead. Then Dawson gave me back the docket I'd signed three weeks earlier, and left us alone.

'We're like the Ancient Mariner,' remarked George, as we made preparations to leave. 'Doomed for ever to carry that trolley around.'

While all this was happening, other UniVans had been busily coming and going from Merry Park. The frenetic late-morning activity had brought John Jones to his gatehouse door, and he now stood motionless at the top of the steps, surveying the yard below. This was John's favoured position when the weather allowed. As usual, his hands were resting on the safety rail and he appeared to be gazing at nothing in particular. When we headed for the gateway, however, I saw him raise one finger, ever so slightly. Then he put his hands in his pockets and went back inside.

'Hello,' I said. 'John wants me for something.'

I stopped the van, got out, and went up the steps. John was now sitting on the edge of his desk, staring at the lino.

'A word in your shell-like,' he said. 'Close the door, will you?'

10

It was an isolated world that John Jones occupied here, high up above the yard, but nonetheless it had its advantages. At his fingertips were all the requisites for his daily vigil: kettle, toaster and teapot, as well as a good selection of newspapers. The gatehouse was an airy structure, rather like a signal box without any levers. From the windows he had a commanding view of not only the depot, but also the leafy park on the one side, and the sports field on the other. The light that streamed in during the summer months was so intense that it would have been easy for John to grow tomatoes, or even orchids, if he so desired, though for reasons of his own he'd chosen not to. He lived a peaceful existence, undisturbed by casual visitors, and, as far as I knew, he was answerable to no one. The job of a gatekeeper was to ensure that the only vehicles entering or leaving the premises were UniVans, and it allowed him some degree of autonomy. Yet despite his apparent aloofness, John was always first to hear any news or rumours that were circulating around The Scheme. This was partly due to the internal telephone system, which linked him directly to every other gatehouse in the network. It was a common sight to see John standing at his window, holding the phone to his ear as he absorbed the latest piece of information. He also received gossip first-hand by inviting select individuals into his domain. The signal for such an invitation was the discreetly raised finger I'd seen a little earlier. There would then follow a brief conversation during which John would learn a lot, and reveal a little. When I came up the steps I expected our meeting to take the same form, so I was surprised to discover that the prime purpose of my visit was for *him* to tell *me* something.

'It's about our friend Mr Gosling,' he announced.

'Oh, yes?'

'I've heard from a certain quarter that it was your duty card that led to his recent downfall.'

'Well, yes,' I said. 'But it wasn't my fault. Nesbitt got hold of the card and saw all those signatures on it.'

'That's what I heard.'

'Is there a problem then?'

'Not if we're careful, no.'

John took a step towards the window, and stood looking out. Down below, in the yard, groups of men were gathered around their vans discussing the matters of the day.

'Our friend Mr Gosling,' he continued, 'seems to have stirred up a lot of sentiment in the ranks, one way or the other. Expect you've heard the talk. Some parties see him as a munificent benefactor, while others regard him as an agent of sloth. I've got a feeling the whole issue is going to erupt very soon, and if that duty card comes to light people might jump to the wrong conclusion.'

'Blimey,' I murmured. 'I hadn't thought of that.'

'Well, you ought to,' said John, turning at last to face me. 'You could be stuck right in the middle of it all.'

'Yes.'

He lowered his voice. 'Fortunately, the card in question appears to have gone missing, so there's no written evidence.'

'That's a relief.'

'You might find it useful to have a look behind the fire hose at Long Reach, if you get my drift.'

'Oh, right,' I said. 'Thanks, John. That's one I owe you.'

'My pleasure,' he replied. 'Perhaps you could get our friend George to drop off one of his cakes sometime.'

'Of course. Er . . . any idea what's going to become of Gosling?'

As soon as I'd asked the question I knew I shouldn't have. John gave a long sigh and shook his head.

'Don't ask me things like that,' he said. 'It's more than my job's worth.'

Next moment I was being shown the door. Again I thanked him for his advice and he told me to think nothing of it. Then, as John settled into his swivel chair, I went back down the steps to rejoin George.

'What was all that about?' he enquired, when I got into the van.

'Don't ask,' I said. 'Just drop him off a cake sometime, can you?'

'OK then.'

Luckily George wasn't the prying kind, so he pursued the matter no further. On the subject of cakes, his main concern was fitting tomorrow's arrangements around the mass meeting at Merry Park. His life was a constant logistical puzzle to which he had to adjust daily. Now, as we continued our journey, he sat in the dummy seat with a notebook and pencil, working out the best solution.

'I think we'll have to give Sandro a miss for the next day or two,' he declared at length. 'Spread the load so we don't get a backlog building up again. While we're at Blackwell I'll speak to Osgood and find out if he can hold a couple of boxes overnight. Oh, and that reminds me: I need to get in touch with Pete Giggs to see what his next few duties are . . .'

And so it went on. George had only been on The Scheme for two years, but in that short time he'd built up a system within a system, an entire structure whose sole purpose was to facilitate the distribution of cakes. I often wondered why he hadn't gone into business, instead of just riding round with me all day long.

When we returned to Long Reach that evening I

asked Horsefall what I should do with the pallet trolley we'd picked up earlier.

'Don't ask me,' he said helpfully.

'Can't I leave it here?'

'No you can't. We've already got one. Where did it come from originally?'

'Cotton Town.'

'So take it back there.'

'But we won't be going that way for weeks,' I said. 'We've only just started a new duty.'

'Well, leave it in your van for the time being,' he suggested. 'It's not getting in the way is it?'

'No, suppose not.'

'There you are then. Problem solved.'

With a self-satisfied look on his face, Horsefall strolled over to his office and began preparing to close up for the night. During the few minutes I'd been talking to him most of the other staff had clocked out. George had already gone, and now there was practically no one around. I remained on the loading bay a little longer. Then, when I was completely alone, I went to the fire hose and looked behind it. Lodged between the housing and the wall was a duty card. I retrieved it, cast my eye over the myriad of signatures, and tore it into tiny little pieces.

The Scheme had never witnessed a mass meeting before, simply because there'd been no need for one. Not once in its history had there been any cause for dissatisfaction: we were well paid; we were immune to commercial fluctuation; and the job itself was a cinch. We merely had to drive a van between A, B and C, and our continued employment was guaranteed. It had been like that for almost three decades, without one word of complaint. Now, however, discontent had arisen, and I was curious to find out what would be the outcome.

As we approached Merry Park next day, the first thing we noticed was the huge number of UniVans lined along the approach road. They were nose to tail on the kerbside, right up to the gate, and most of them bore the letter g insignia. Many more were crammed into the yard, although the loading bay had been left clear, presumably to allow for scheduled vehicles to operate as normal. I backed in and switched off the engine, aware of the sheer volume of people milling around everywhere. We waited a while in case anyone offered to unload us, but as the minutes ticked by this seemed increasingly unlikely, so eventually we gave up and joined the throng. There appeared to be a general movement towards a point at the far side of the yard, where I could see Billy Barker standing on some kind of platform, along with a man I hadn't seen before. As a matter of fact, I only recognized about a third of the total number present, these being workers from the depots we visited regularly. The rest, I presumed, were from outlying parts of the region, and I had to admit that the large turnout was most impressive.

'Are these all swervers?' asked George, as we worked our way through the crowd.

'Suppose so,' I replied. 'Hello, looks like they're starting.'

We could now see that Billy's platform was actually a large empty crate. He stood talking to his companion, nodding his head in apparent agreement over something, and then taking a loud-hailer that had been handed up to him. There was a widespread stir of anticipation, followed by polite silence.

'Well, everyone,' he began, in a voice loud yet fuzzy. 'Thank you for coming along today. I think you all know how important this issue is, and why it's necessary to make a stand.'

This brought a murmur of assent from the onlookers, which in turn boosted Billy's confidence so that he no longer felt the need to shout into the loud-hailer. When he resumed, the fuzziness had lessened.

'At the outset of the campaign we decided to hold a general meeting, and invite someone who could fully articulate our concerns; to put them into perspective, so to speak. I'm sure you'll agree that Les Prentice was by far the best choice. Les is going to share one or two thoughts with us, and hopefully point us in the right direction. He's journeyed here especially from Royal Pond, and needs to be back there fairly sharp this afternoon, so, without further ado, could you join me in welcoming Les Prentice! A big hand please! Les.'

A cheer rose up as Billy passed the loud-hailer to the other man, before stepping down off the platform. A quick glance around told me that the gathering had swollen somewhat during the past few minutes, with new arrivals turning up all the time. I also noticed John Jones watching proceedings from the privacy of his gatehouse. There was no sign, though, of any supers or other Scheme officials. Clearly they'd decided to maintain a low profile.

Everyone's attention was now on Les Prentice, who had a very relaxed look about him. As far as I could see he had no notes to read from, but nevertheless it soon became obvious that he was quite used to public speaking.

'Eight hours,' he said, addressing the space above our heads. 'Doesn't sound a lot, does it?' He paused with a quizzical expression on his face, as if examining the thought. Then he continued. 'Oh no, eight hours doesn't seem anything at all. Not until you consider that it's a third of a day. Yes, my friends, one third of your life spent behind the wheel of a UniVan, or perched on a forklift truck!'

As this fact sunk in, a sort of groan of recognition spread through the crowd, and I realized all at once that Les had his audience captivated.

'Think about it,' he went on. 'We're expected to rise from our beds at seven in the morning in order to arrive at work on time, which means we're getting up in darkness during the winter months. And it's almost dark again when we go home! Toiling from dawn until dusk! What other industry would demand that of a loyal workforce? What other industry has men going round and round, as if they were on a treadmill, for eight consecutive hours? Only our glorious Scheme could come up with something like that! Only our glorious, glorious Scheme!'

Les paused again.

'Not that we've ever held a grievance, of course. We know as well as anyone that we need to do a reasonable day's work for a reasonable day's pay. But that's the key word, isn't it? Reasonable. We're reasonable men, and for the most part we turn up, week in, week out, and do eight full hours without demur. And all we ask in return is the odd glimmer of gold amongst the chaff; the occasional day in clover. My friends, let me say this to you: we're not demanding a life of ease; we're not even against the principle of the flat day. We simply want what's fair. That signature at the bottom of a card can turn a relentless slog into an enjoyable excursion, but just lately it's become a positive rarity! No one can deny that the incidence of early swerves has been greatly reduced over the past few weeks. What we're witnessing here is the gradual erosion of our established customs and practices. And if we continue to tolerate such a process, then how long before the spectre of compulsory overtime raises its head?!'

The roar of agreement that went up when Les said this made me think he was about to be swept aloft by the multitude. Instead, he raised a hand for silence, and spoke again.

'The ice we're on is thinner than it looks. We should make known our misgivings before it's too late, and there are any number of options open to us. Perhaps, for example, we could consider implementing a go-slow strategy.'

'Well, no one could go much slower than you, Les!'

This bit of good-natured heckling, which came from someone over at the right-hand side, produced a ripple of laughter and made Les himself smile broadly. When he tried to resume, however, there was a second interruption.

'Where's Mr Gosling in your hour of need?!'

Such a deliberate taunt could only have come from a flat-dayer, and I peered about me in an attempt to see who it was. The comment had obviously rattled a few members of the crowd, who raised their voices in objection, but then someone else began shouting, 'We want eight!' over and over again. Quickly this was taken up by several other people, all chanting in unison, and I realized that the meeting had been infiltrated. The chants grew louder and louder, while the early swervers tried their very best to drown them out with jeers and whistles.

'You can shout all you like!' declared a high-pitched voice behind me. 'But you'll soon be hoarse!'

Turning round I saw Martin from Eden Lacy.

'Hello, Martin!' I said, struggling to make myself heard above the din. 'What are you doing here?'

'Well, I thought I'd better come and find out what all the fuss was about.'

Quickly I introduced him to George, who seemed untroubled by the turn of events. Then Martin told us that the flat-dayers had disrupted a number of other meetings he'd attended.

'The extremists are the worst,' he said. 'They've forsworn their ten-off-the-eight, and now they think everyone else should do the same. Caused pandemonium at Riverhead depot, by all accounts.'

'Blimey,' I remarked. 'You're certainly well-informed.'

'You have to be, don't you, the way things have been going lately?'

'So which way do your sympathies lie?'

'Neither way,' said Martin. 'I'm a strictly neutral observer.'

Our conversation went no further, because at this point a UniVan came into the yard and began nosing its way through the margins of the crowd in a very obstinate manner. Above it fluttered a huge flag emblazoned with an enclosed figure eight, and the driver kept sounding his horn to make people move aside. Then he insisted on reversing onto the bay, where his assistant got out, opened the roller door and stood waiting to be unloaded. I looked at my watch. It was now one thirty. Right on cue, a couple of superintendents approached from the direction of the main offices. Not long after that the meeting broke up and the swervers began drifting slowly back to work. We could hear them complaining to one another about the outrageous audacity of the flat-dayers. The dozen or so interlopers had slipped away during the confusion caused by the arrival of the rogue UniVan, and now Billy Barker, Les Prentice and their associates stood holding a postmortem. Whether the gathering had been a success or a failure was impossible to know. True, Les was a gifted orator and he'd succeeded in putting the main points across, but beyond that the outcome was indecisive.

As George and I wandered back to our vehicle there appeared to be only one absolute certainty: The Scheme for Full Employment was on the verge of a schism.

11

On Friday morning I found a note attached to the windscreen of UV55. It was from George, asking me to collect all remaining cakes from the engineers' workshop, and then pick him up outside the depot gates. Some things never changed. I left Chris Peachment loading the van and went over to see Rob Marshall.

'I'll be glad to see the back of this lot,' he said, leading me inside. 'We haven't been able to use our workbench for weeks.'

The bench in question was piled with about fifteen cake boxes, and when we began moving them we found several slips of paper hidden underneath. These comprised unused worksheets, collision damage reports and order forms for vehicle spare parts. Also an internal memorandum. It was printed in red letters and said:

Rob glanced at the memo.

'Ah, yes,' he said. 'I wondered where that had gone.'

'What's a weight test?' I asked.

'Well, I thought you of all people would know,' he replied. 'Being a bit of an enthusiast, like.'

'What are you talking about? I'm not an enthusiast. Never have been. They're all barmy, that lot.'

'Alright, but you can't say you're not interested in UniVans.'

'Only for professional reasons,' I insisted. 'Now what's all this about a weight test?'

'It all goes back to when The Scheme first started up,' Rob explained. 'They'd already built about two thousand vans when they realized the unladen weight wasn't compatible with the axles they were using.'

'Dear oh dear. I bet Sir Ronald Thompson wasn't very pleased about that.'

'I'll say he wasn't. And to be honest I think that's what finished him. You know: all the worry.'

'So did they go back and start again?'

'Ooh no, they couldn't do that. There was too much at stake. Don't forget, The Scheme had been put forward as the great panacea: everything depended on its success. They needed a quick solution, and they came up with this provisional arrangement where they'd continue using the axles as long as they didn't break. That was almost thirty years ago, and so far they've been alright, but the other part of the compromise was they had to weigh a vehicle at random, once a year.'

'I thought they all weighed the same.'

'They do,' said Rob. 'It's just a formality really: a sort of ritual to demonstrate they're keeping their eye on the job.'

'And the honour falls to Long Reach this year?'

'Yep,' he nodded. 'Blinking nuisance. It means we've got to set a UniVan to one side just so it can be weighed.'

That wasn't for another few weeks, of course. In the meantime, I had to transfer fifteen cakes to our van without anyone noticing. While Rob watched to make sure the coast was clear, I made three journeys with my arms full and placed the boxes in the cab. Then, quietly cursing George, I went back up onto the loading bay.

I knew Chris had finished putting the goods on board because I could see him at the far end of the depot, dealing with another vehicle. He'd left the van's roller door open, however, and when I glanced inside I was surprised to see Joyce standing there. She was gazing at one of the crates and seemed to be totally preoccupied, as if its contents held a great significance. What, I wondered, was she thinking about? In the gloom of the van's interior she appeared somehow different, the dim half-light having softened her features considerably. This made her seem quite approachable, vulnerable even, and it was with a certain tenderness that I broke the silence and spoke:

'You lost something?'

Joyce peered at me briefly, then returned her gaze to the crate. 'No,' she replied. 'I was just looking to see what was going to Merry Park today. According to the labels you're taking four hundred windscreen wipers and five gross of rear reflectors.'

'That's what I like to hear,' I said. 'A substantial cargo of indispensable goods, all winging their way from depot to depot.'

'Ridiculous, isn't it?' said Joyce, now turning to face me. 'This Scheme's a complete sham.'

I stared at her in disbelief. 'But it's the centrepin of our economic system!'

'Nonsense!' she snapped. 'It's nothing more than a sideshow! A relic from some bygone age when people didn't know any better, dreamt up by do-gooders in their ivory towers! It's inefficient, expensive and wasteful, and what it needs is a thorough shake-up! These vans should be made to earn their keep instead of going round and round full of unwanted spare parts. The depots should be put to proper commercial use, and the staff paid by results. Otherwise this entire outfit will go exactly the same way as all those other failed social experiments, like public transport, school dinners and municipal orchestras!'

When she'd ceased speaking Joyce stood looking at me with a challenging expression on her face, as if daring me to contradict her.

'Don't they serve school dinners any more then?' I asked.

She shook her head slowly. 'Not if I had my way, they wouldn't.'

Without another word she stalked past me and approached her office, leaving me to recover from the onslaught. Obviously she saw The Scheme very differently from me, but at the same time she seemed quite passionate about its future wellbeing. This suggested I could look forward to further conversations on the subject.

The time now being eight fifteen, I closed the roller door, jumped in the van and got going. At the first corner after the gate I saw George. He was waiting beside a low wall, on top of which rested a large wooden tray laden with cakes. I pulled up, and between us we loaded them into the cab.

'How many's that altogether?' I asked.

'Twenty-six,' he replied. 'All bound for Sandro's.'

'How come there's so many all of a sudden?'

'It's not all of a sudden. It's just a gradual expansion of business.'

'So what are you going to do when there's no more room in the cab?'

'Well,' said George. 'I'll have to think of an alternative arrangement, won't I?'

He spent the entire journey to Merry Park looking very uncomfortable, perched amongst the pile of boxes.

'Don't forget you promised a cake for John Jones,' I reminded him, as we passed beneath the gatehouse.

'No, alright,' he said. 'But not today: these are all spoken for.'

After Merry Park he was forced to remain under the teetering stack all the way to Blackwell, then a further two miles along the Ring Road. Only when we pulled up outside Sandro's Bakery was his ordeal over. For a moment I was tempted to let him carry them all in on his own, but in the end I relented and gave him a hand. Even so, it took several journeys just to get the boxes into the kitchen, and then Sandro had to find somewhere to store them all.

'Maybe I should get bigger premises,' he remarked. 'For all this extra trade you're bringing.'

As a matter of fact, Sandro already seemed to be preparing for expansion. Since our previous visit his staff had been augmented by a new assistant, a man in a white apron and cap who was busy removing loaves of bread from the oven. He appeared unused to the work and was sweating heavily, but nonetheless he continued his labours while George and I stood talking to Sandro. Only when he'd completed his task and closed the oven door did he finally turn round. It was Gosling.

The moment he saw us he wilted visibly, and we had to dash over and sit him down on a chair. Then we made him put his head between his legs, while Sandro fetched a glass of water. Not until another minute had elapsed did he recover sufficiently to speak.

'Sorry about that,' he said. 'I'll be alright now, thanks.'

'What are you doing here?' I asked. 'I thought you were suspended on full pay.'

'I was,' he replied. 'But to tell the truth, once Nesbitt's enquiry had started my position became untenable. I more or less had to leave. Then Sandro kindly offered me employment, and I accepted.'

'But you're not a trained baker,' said George. 'It'll kill you.'

'He's only learning the ropes for a few days,' Sandro assured us. 'Then I'm going to have him icing the cakes. He has a very artistic hand.'

'Really?'

'Oh yes. Even his signature is elegant.'

The innocent way in which Sandro made this last remark suggested he had no idea of the tumult that Gosling's signature had caused over the past few weeks. Indeed, to most outsiders The Scheme probably looked much the same as ever, with hordes of UniVans going about their normal daily business. The public knew nothing of the division and strife that was threatening to tear it apart. Some passers-by may have been vaguely curious about the mass meetings that had taken place of late, but such events were usually over within an hour and for the most part attracted scant attention. The same went for the rival insignias which were now being displayed on virtually every vehicle. In the eyes of the opposing factions these represented highly important principles, yet they must have been completely meaningless to the casual observer.

Closer scrutiny, however, would have revealed further signs of internal conflict. Many Scheme employees had recently taken to wearing lapel badges which indicated at a glance whether they were flat-dayers or swervers (the 'early' having been dropped from everyday use). Some of the latter group took their allegiance a little further, and went round with duty cards sticking out of their breast pockets. This earned the derision of the flat-dayers, who were all rather strait-laced and not given to such vulgar ostentation. They preferred a low-key approach, going about their duties in strict accordance with the rule book, then clocking off in solemn silence at the end of the working day.

And, of course, neither side spoke to the other. The time for judicious debate and mutual understanding had passed. Instead, there now existed a stony silence between two parties that each believed in the correctness of its purpose. Which made the smooth running of The Scheme increasingly difficult. Again and again there were instances of flat-day warehousemen refusing to unload drivers they suspected of being 'swerve-minded'. Such action invariably had a knock-on effect, causing further delays throughout the network. Yet if you were to talk to anyone directly involved in these disputes, they could present any number of plausible arguments to prove their case. Taken in isolation, both schools of thought appeared to possess a reasoned and balanced outlook. It was only when they were set against one another that their intransigence was exposed.

An added complication lay in the fact that the flat-dayers were hopelessly divided amongst themselves. True, they occupied the higher moral ground because they adhered to the eight hours on which The Scheme was based. They were effectively split, however, between those who'd given up the ten-off-the-eight and those who hadn't. Their cause, as a result, suffered from an inherent weakness. The ten-off-the-eight was a long-standing managerial concession, but a minority of extremists had sacrificed it for the sake of principle. This left a frustrated majority who accused them of 'selling themselves down the river'. The larger group tended to congregate around the automatic vehicle wash, which they monopolized for those crucial ten minutes at the end of the day. The extremists, meanwhile, made a big show of working right up to the bell.

At the opposite end of the spectrum were the swervers, whose position was built on a vague notion of 'fairness' and little more. They argued that the flat day was never intended as a rigid code. Instead it should be regarded as a flexible guide, with working hours being allowed to vary according to daily requirements. Needless to say, this was a romantic notion: strictly speaking, they didn't have a leg to stand on.

Nonetheless, over the next couple of weeks we began to hear reports that swerves were being dished out once more. These rumours remained unsubstantiated for a short time, and then one afternoon Bryan Tovey arrived back at the yard a good hour before the rest of us. His card had been signed by a super from Rudgeway depot. After that, early finishes started to become more common again, and it seemed that things were returning to normal. Perhaps Les Prentice's threat of a go-slow had achieved the desired effect, or maybe the management had simply decided that the recent curbs led to more trouble than they were worth.

Whatever the reason, I for one was glad that the hostilities were over and we could begin to enjoy life on The Scheme again. I hadn't really liked seeing my colleagues falling out with each other, and hoped, for example, that Bill and Richard Harper would soon be able to resolve their differences. This appeared highly likely when I saw them both one evening, standing by the punch clock and chatting quite amicably. Next morning, however, I turned up at work to see a UniVan blocking the gate so that no other vehicle could get in or out. Then I bumped into George.

'What's going on?' I asked.

'They've called a strike,' he replied.

'But they can't have!' I said. 'They've got their swerves back. What more do they want?'

'Oh no,' said George. 'It's not the swervers this time. It's the flat-dayers.'

Apparently they'd decided that the only way to save the eight-hour day was to go on strike and bring the matter to public attention. Similar action was taking place right across The Scheme, although the supers had made it clear that anybody who wanted to work would be allowed to.

George looked at me. 'What are we going to do then?'

'Not sure.'

'No, nor me.'

'Tell you what,' I said. 'Go and see Arthur for the keys and we'll sit in the van and have a think about it.'

'Righto then.'

He headed inside through the swing doors as I continued across the yard. The whole of the loading bay was lined with UniVans, while yet more were parked on the standing area opposite. All had their engines switched off, and I suddenly became aware of how quiet the whole place was. Normally at this time of the morning there was no end of activity going on as the forklifts buzzed about getting everyone loaded. Today, though, there were just groups of men standing round looking aimless. UV55 was waiting where I'd left it the previous evening, halfway along the bay, so I wandered up and stood leaning against its side. After a couple of minutes, George came back.

'Our mind's been made up for us,' he announced. 'Arthur's on strike and he won't issue any keys.'

So there we all were: flat-dayers, swervers, everybody: the whole lot of us marooned at Long Reach and unable to work whether we wanted to or not. I guessed the situation must be the same at all the other depots, because even if the keymasters weren't on strike then likely as not the fuel attendants would be. Or the forklift men. Or the duty clerks. Every job depended on every other job, but now the entire Scheme had ground to a halt.

'How am I going to get my cakes out?' George demanded.

'Don't know,' I replied. 'How many have you got outstanding?'

'None at the moment,' he said. 'But you've seen how quickly the backlog can build up. I could really do with getting back to work as quickly as possible.'

Something told me George would be disappointed on this count. If the flat-dayers wanted their strike to be effective then surely it would have to be of some length, and I now began to think we might be in for a protracted dispute. I also wondered how many people had considered the full implications of the strike. All along the bay, and down in the yard, I could see crews standing next to their UniVans as if expecting matters to be settled within the next couple of hours. Some of them were passing the time by polishing their headlamps. Others simply lounged in the morning sunshine. Few seemed aware that they may be stuck here for quite a while.

At the far end of the bay I noticed Jonathan, to whom I hadn't spoken for a few weeks. I knew, however, that he'd recently completed his term as a floating assistant driver, and had now teamed up on a permanent basis with Peter Lawrence. When he spotted me and George he came over.

'Marvellous, isn't it?' he said. 'I've only just joined The Scheme and I'm already on strike.'

'Are you a flat-dayer then?' I asked.

'Not really, but Peter is.'

'Yes, I thought he would be.'

'So I'm just going along with it, sort of thing. I suppose they'll be sending us home soon, will they?'

'Why?'

'Well, we can't do anything useful here, can we?'

'No,' I replied. 'But you don't qualify for strike pay unless you remain on the premises for the full eight hours.'

'What!' exclaimed George, plainly dismayed.

'Blimey,' said Jonathan. 'I didn't know there was any provision for strike pay.'

'There's provision for everything,' I said. 'I remember Bill Harper telling me all about it when I first started. Not that they've ever had any call for it, of course.'

'Until now,' said George.

'Yes,' I agreed. 'Until now.'

At the realization that he was going to have to hang around all day, George began to look gloomy.

'Eight hours!' he said. 'I bet the extremists are delighted about that!'

I looked at the clock and saw that it had ticked round to eight forty-five. On any other morning we'd be out on the road by this time, heading towards Merry Park, or Cotton Town, or wherever else our duty took us. Today, though, we were going nowhere, and all of a sudden four thirty seemed a long way away.

Inside the superintendents' office I could see Horsefall, Collis and Meeks, all sitting round the desk with their heads down. It was going to be a difficult period for them too, and doubtless they were doing their best not to be seen throwing their weight around at this early stage. Besides, I'd long held the opinion that the supers were more interested in keeping each other in line than dealing with the requirements of The Scheme itself, a point which had been amply demonstrated during the Gosling episode. Presumably they'd decided to remain aloof and let the flat-dayers and the swervers sort things out amongst themselves. Joyce, I noticed, was nowhere to be seen.

'Fancy a round of darts?' Jonathan suggested.

George shook his head. 'I've already had a look in the games room. There's a queue just to get onto the board.'

'How about going up the canteen?'

'No thanks,' I said. 'It's far too noisy for me.'

'Aw, come on,' said George. 'You can't stay down here all day.'

'But it's ages since I've been up there,' I protested. 'I'll feel out of place.'

'All the more reason to go there then.'

He would brook no further argument, so the three of us trooped through the swing doors and up the back stairs. Even as we approached the canteen I could hear the clash of newly-rinsed cutlery being thrown into the racks by the catering staff, while plates were noisily washed, dried and stacked for immediate use.

'Why can't they learn to do that quietly?' I murmured.

'Oh, stop moaning,' said George, pushing open another pair of swing doors and leading us inside.

It seemed that half the workforce had had the same idea as us. At almost every table there were groups of men sitting talking, drinking tea or enjoying an extended mid-morning breakfast. In most cases all three at once. Yet I could see straightaway that the flat-dayers and the swervers were having nothing to do with one another. They sat at separate tables, each party acting for all the world as if the other didn't exist. The only contact would be when a sauce bottle or salt cellar needed to be passed from one table to the next, at which time a sort of icy politeness would accompany the transaction.

We sent Jonathan to the counter to buy the teas, then George and I found an empty table and sat down. Across the aisle from us were Ron Curtain, Derek Moss and Dave Cuthbert. They were all flat-dayers, and were sitting behind a small oblong sign that said STRIKE COMMITTEE in bold letters. Derek had a list of names in front of him and was going through them with a biro, putting a tick here and there. He gave me a nod as we took our seats, then resumed his examination of the list. A minute later we were joined by Jonathan.

'That all looks very serious,' he said, lowering his voice somewhat. 'Do you suppose it's a list of striking flat-dayers?'

'Could be,' I answered. 'On the other hand it might be a list of non-striking swervers.'

'Hardly makes any difference either way,' remarked George. 'We're all stuck in the same boat.'

He put three spoonfuls of sugar into his tea and sat stirring it in a disconsolate manner. Meanwhile, I pondered whether I should go to the counter and order some breakfast now, or leave it for a couple of hours and call it dinner. To tell the truth I had no appetite as I hadn't done any work yet, so in the end I decided to wait.

We'd finished our teas and been back for seconds when Bryan Tovey came and presented himself before the strike committee. He'd been sitting at a table over at the far side of the canteen, talking earnestly to a group of fellow swervers, when suddenly we'd seen him rise from his seat and march purposefully across the room. Now he stood gazing down at Derek, Ron and Dave.

'Don't mind my asking,' he asked. 'But who authorized you to hold this strike, exactly?'

'It was a majority decision,' Derek replied.

'You had a vote then, did you?'

'We had a show of hands, yes.'

'When?'

'Last night after you lot had gone home.'

'We also consulted several esteemed persons,' added Dave. 'People like John Ford and Len Walker. They both gave the strike their full approval.'

'I see,' said Bryan. 'And that justifies keeping us stranded here all day, does it?'

'Of course it does,' said Dave. 'It's necessary for the greater good of The Scheme.'

The sheer earnestness of this statement seemed to throw Bryan slightly, and he lapsed into silence for a moment, apparently lost for words.

And then a more general silence spread through the canteen. One of the swing doors had been opened slightly, and in the gap a head had appeared. It belonged to Ray Coppin. When we all looked in his direction he gave us a wan smile, and withdrew again.

12

The first day of the strike was the longest I could ever remember. By 11 A.M., time was dragging so slowly that I'd become convinced the clock on the wall had stopped altogether. Only when the big hand ticked forward by one minute did I realize I was wrong.

Having now consumed four mugs of tea apiece, George, Jonathan and I sat listening to the surrounding hubbub of voices engaged in ceaseless debate. Never had I heard so many people concur with one another so wholeheartedly, while at the same time totally disagreeing with their colleagues at the neighbouring tables. Why no one came to blows was a miracle, since there was hardly room in that canteen for two opposing forces. Instead, a perpetual stand-off existed, in which they all grumbled about how blinkered and unreasonable the other side was, compared to their own enlightened selves. Needless to say, I'd listened to all the arguments a hundred times before and didn't need to hear them recited once again. Eventually, therefore, I decided I'd had enough and went back downstairs, leaving George and Jonathan to join the queue for darts.

On passing the key room I noticed the door was ajar, so I gave it a gentle push and saw Arthur sitting inside reading a newspaper.

'Oh, it's you,' he said, looking up. 'I'm closed.'

'I know,' I replied. 'But I was just wondering if I could borrow my van's keys for a few minutes.'

'What for?'

'Well, I thought I'd stick it in the vehicle wash. Smarten it up, sort of thing.'

'I'm afraid the answer's no,' said Arthur. 'We're on strike . . . or hadn't you heard?'

'Yes, but it would only be for a short while. Then I'd bring them back.'

'Look,' he said. 'If I lent you the keys I'd have to lend them to everybody else who came along here on some whim. I've just told you I'm closed. That's why the hatch is down. If you want to wash your van you'll have to get a bucket and mop and do it by hand.'

'Where do I get those from then?'

'Try the janitor.'

'Oh, right, thanks, Arthur. Sorry to bother you.'

He grunted and shut the door behind me as I left. When I got to the janitor's cubbyhole, however, I found it was locked, and I could see no one behind the frosted glass. Then I realized the janitor was most likely on strike, same as everyone else. Arthur had probably sent me there just to get rid of me. Nevertheless, the idea of washing my van was now firmly stuck in my head, so I began wandering around the depot in search of a bucket and mop. When this proved fruitless I crossed the yard to the engineers' workshop. Surely, I thought, they would have something on hand to deal with the occasional oil spillage.

I entered through the door we'd used when collecting George's cakes over the past few weeks, but there was no sign of Rob Marshall, or any of the others. Silence reigned. Venturing further inside, I passed Ken Scanlon's empty office, and then went into the workshop proper. This had no windows and was lit entirely by long fluorescent strips, suspended from the ceiling on thin brass chains. The building was deserted, but the sight I beheld brought me to an abrupt halt. There in front of me, raised up on the hydraulic ramp, was a half-assembled UniVan. Its wheels, panels, roof and cab had been removed, leaving only the chassis and the engine in place, with the headlights standing naked on their stalks. Scattered all around were replacement parts, as well as screwdrivers, wrenches and spanners, the job having apparently been abandoned the moment the strike began. An inspection lamp had been clipped onto the chassis, with crocodile teeth to keep it firmly in position. This cast a harsh glow over the stricken vehicle, and seeing it in such a reduced state caused me to feel an odd twinge of sadness, as if something cherished was about to be lost for ever. I stood for several moments absorbing the poignant scene. Then I left the workshop and went back out into the sunshine.

It was a warm day, and by now quite a few people had come down to the yard from the canteen. They were stretching their legs by strolling around in groups of two or three. I still hadn't got hold of a bucket and mop, but these increased numbers began to make me think I should forget the whole notion of washing my van. After all, it wouldn't really have done for me to be seen working in the middle of a dispute, especially when such important events were unfolding all around me. The fact that I was neither a swerver nor a flat-dayer was irrelevant. This was the first strike in the entire history of The Scheme, and I realized I would have to go along with it whether I liked it or not.

The extremists, I soon discovered, took a completely different view. I'd assumed they'd be fully supportive of the flat-dayers' action, so I was surprised when I heard that a group of them had taken over and occupied the games room. Their purpose was not to play darts, or cards, or snooker, however, but rather to protest against the strike. The news was broken to me by Dave Whelan.

'They've barricaded themselves inside,' he said. 'Blinking spoilsports. Now we've got nothing to do at all.'

It seemed the occupation had been led by Richard Harper, whose followers believed the strike would turn national opinion against us. Moreover, they strongly objected to people enjoying the pursuit of leisure at such a critical time. The Strike Committee had asked Bill to try and make his brother see reason, but so far his efforts had been to no avail.

The early swervers, meanwhile, were highly equivocal about their attitude towards the strike. By their very nature, of course, they were inclined to welcome the idea of a few hours lounging around doing nothing, since this was how many of them spent their afternoons anyway. It was one thing, though, for a driver to pass his time parked in some discreet lay-by several miles from the depot. It was quite another to be confined within its bounds. And so it was that when three o'clock came and went, the swervers began to look increasingly uncomfortable. Normally around this time they would be making plans to waylay some unsuspecting super with the hope of getting their cards signed. Today, by contrast, they had no alternative but to wait until four thirty.

The last ten minutes were the longest of all. There was no question of claiming the ten-off-the-eight because it didn't apply during a strike. Besides, the vans hadn't been anywhere all day so there were no keys to hand in. Even so, the irony of the moment was lost on none of us, and I noticed a good few heads being shaken with sad resignation. At twenty past four, those who'd remained all day in the canteen came down and joined the crowd that was massing near the gates. At four twenty-nine the extremists emerged from the games room, taking care to padlock the door behind them so they could continue their occupation the next morning. Then finally, at half past four on the dot, we all left the premises, cheering as we went. At long last we could go home.

The next major development came a couple of days later when the canteen ladies decided to join the strike. Apparently, they'd had enough of serving tea to hordes of ungrateful men who did nothing but sit around the tables and talk. Their action, needless to say, put the flat-dayers into a quandary, as they clearly hadn't bargained for such a turn of events. Indeed, some of them were overheard trying to dissuade the ladies from striking, no doubt hoping to preserve their supply of subsidized food and drink. They did not meet with success, however, and by the end of the first week the kitchen shutters were down. Fortunately, the Strike Committee managed to requisition a tea urn, so for the time being at least the threatened privations were kept to a minimum.

On the following Monday the depot received a visit from Nesbitt. He appeared while Jonathan and I were sitting on the edge of the loading bay, watching an impromptu game of football that was going on in the middle of the yard. Such matches had come to be frequent events as the strike wore on, and invariably took place between teams composed of swervers on the one side and flat-dayers on the other. The score was nil–nil when Jonathan nudged me and pointed to a figure in black, walking slowly round the periphery.

'Blimey,' I said. 'It's boiling hot weather and he's still wearing his full uniform.'

Nesbitt had now come to a halt and was gazing across at the footballers, none of whom had noticed him.

'I wonder what he wants,' said Jonathan.

'Probably just having a nose about,' I suggested. 'Something to occupy him while he thinks up new ways of foiling the swervers.'

'Well, it takes one to catch one.'

'How do you mean?'

'When Nesbitt was a driver he was the worst swerver of them all.'

'Who told you that?'

'Bloke I met over at Rudgeway depot. He used to know someone who worked with Nesbitt in the early days of The Scheme. Never did a full day for weeks on end, by all accounts. Got his card signed on a regular basis. Apparently the management were quite pleased when he applied to be a super. It meant they'd got him on their side.'

'Who was this bloke then?'

'Oh, I don't know his name. But he assured me the story was true.'

There came a huge roar from the middle of the yard. The flat-dayers had just scored an own goal, and the swervers were running round congratulating one another as if they were taking part in the Cup Final itself. By the time play was resumed, Nesbitt had moved on.

We never did find out the exact reason for his being at Long Reach. Nor did I verify Jonathan's story, and I eventually dismissed it as a piece of unfounded gossip. What I didn't realize was that it was just the first of a stream of wild tales that became common currency as the strike progressed. Many of these centred around Gosling, whose continued absence only served to fuel the rumour mill. One such report claimed that he'd been put to work stoking the coal-fired heating system at some far-flung depot. Another said he'd been given the task of sorting through all the used duty cards, separating the ones with signatures from the ones without. The chore would take him several years to complete. Both stories were complete fabrications, of course, I knew that for a fact, but under the circumstances I thought it was probably wiser to say nothing.

Yet there was one rumour that appeared to have some degree of credence. It began circulating sometime during the third week of the strike and I heard it from more than one source. Seemingly, a group of enthusiasts had approached the management and offered to drive the UniVans until the dispute between the two camps was settled. This would be on a strictly voluntary basis, the work being unpaid, and they were ready to start right away. According to the rumour, their offer was 'under consideration'.

Now it should be said that even though the strike was nationwide, it actually had little or no effect on the economic life of the country. It caused no shortages or disruption, and was even welcomed by the majority of road-users, who were no longer impeded by processions of sluggish UniVans. The purpose of the campaign was merely to draw attention to a perceived problem within The Scheme, but the enthusiasts' proposal threatened to expose it to all manner of unwanted scrutiny. After all, if people were prepared to drive UniVans for nothing, then why pay wages to those who weren't?

As a result, the rumour was accompanied by mounting disquiet. I first heard it on one of my rare visits to the canteen, where there had been some recent changes. During the preceding days the Strike Committee had been accused of monopolizing the tea urn, and giving preference to flat-dayers over swervers. Furthermore, they were shown to be thoroughly incompetent, running first out of sugar, then milk, and finally tea itself. At this point George had come forward and offered his services as provisional catering manager, much to the relief of the beleaguered committee, who'd accepted at once. It was his second day in his new role, and I'd decided to go and see how he was getting on. By now the canteen had become a crucible of ideological ferment, and it wasn't long before I'd heard about the enthusiasts volunteering their services. Then I found an empty table and sat down.

'Now as you know,' said a voice nearby. 'It's my opinion that all voluntary work should be banned.'

The speaker was John Ford, whose reputation as

a flat-dayer was well known throughout The Scheme. As usual he was conducting his conversation in the manner of a general forum, addressing his remarks not only to the three companions at his table, but also to anyone else in the vicinity who might be listening. In this he reminded me of a schoolteacher vainly assuming that he had the attention of the whole class. A quick glance round the canteen told me that, in fact, no one was taking the slightest bit of notice of what John had to say, except for his immediate neighbours, and me. This, however, was enough to satisfy him that his words weren't being completely wasted, and when he realised I'd absorbed what he'd said he gave me an appreciative nod.

'Unpaid work has no part to play in a modern economy,' he continued. 'Because if people work for nothing, then you can guarantee that someone somewhere is being put out of a job!'

'So what'll happen if the management accept the enthusiasts' offer?' asked Chris Darling, who was sitting opposite.

'We'll just have to blockade the gates,' John announced, as though the solution was obvious. 'Then there'll be no vans going anywhere.'

Obviously three weeks of strike action had done nothing to blunt John's fervour, and at that moment I realized both sides were still as entrenched as they'd ever been. How long, I wondered, could this deadlock continue? The only person apparently profiting from the situation was George, whose catering operation was in full swing. Yet when I spoke to him a few minutes later, it turned out that even he had problems.

'Sandro's been in touch,' he explained, while pouring me a second mug of tea. 'He wanted to know when we'll be getting back to work so he can start doing Trace's cakes again.'

'What did you tell him?'

'I said I had no idea how long the strike was going on for, and then he told me it was delaying all his plans for expansion. He might even have to lay Gosling off.'

'Oh, we don't want that,' I said. 'Much better for him to stay where he is, out of everyone's sight.'

'I know,' sighed George. 'And I've got Trace pestering me all the time, of course.'

He looked seriously concerned, but I couldn't see any way out of the present impasse. After murmuring a few platitudes about things 'probably sorting themselves out in the long run', I headed back downstairs towards the yard. For some reason I decided to go by way of the main corridor, and when I passed the notice board I saw that a new set of schedules had been posted there. This suggested that the management didn't expect the strike to last indefinitely, and that they were getting on with the everyday business of running The Scheme. On closer examination I was pleased to see that the new duties included journeys to Eden Lacy. It set me wondering how Harold, Martin, Eric and Jim would be coping with the effects of the strike. Did they still pass their days playing cards round that table at the end of the loading bay? And eating platefuls of Martin's sandwiches? Or were they involved in endless debates on the finer points of flat-dayism?

For my part, I had to admit that I was heartily fed up with the strike, and wanted nothing more than to return to work. Oh, how I yearned for those glorious days when we would cruise along the Ring Road, replete with tea and doughnuts, exchanging greetings with our fellow workers, and calling in at depots with proud names like Merry Park, Cotton Town and Rudgeway! Maybe there was a better life to be had than sitting for eight hours behind the wheel of a UniVan, but just at the moment I couldn't think of one.

The door to the duty room swung open and Bob Little emerged, looking most agitated.

'You know what's wrong with this country?' he asked, when he saw me. 'Cooperation, that's what. No one cooperates with anybody else: they just make things as difficult as possible for the next person.'

'I'd never thought of it like that,' I said.

'Well, mark my words, it's true,' said Bob. 'Look at the way this dispute's dragged on and on. It could have been settled to everyone's satisfaction weeks ago if only people would cooperate with one another. Instead, you've got flat-dayers and swervers at loggerheads; you've got supers saying it has nothing to do with them; and you've got the management holding their breath and hoping it'll all go away. Then on top of that there's the enthusiasts waiting like vultures in the rafters. Have you heard what the public are saying about us?'

'No.'

'They're saying we don't know what work is. They're calling us skivers and whingers. Us!! It's diabolical! I can remember when this Scheme was the flagship of industrial society, but these days it's in danger of sinking without a trace!'

Once he'd got it all off his chest, Bob quietened down a bit and told me that the only solution was to put representatives of the two sides in a room together and get them to sort things out. He'd already been on the phone to John Jones at Merry Park, and John had agreed to ring round a few depots to flush out some suitable candidates.

'Les Prentice is a definite,' Bob announced. 'And I think John Ford is another one who could present a balanced view.'

He ran through a list of names, several of which I recognized, and suggested a 'round table' format for the meeting. Jumping at the opportunity of having something to do at last, I immediately offered my assistance in getting the idea off the ground.

'Where are you planning to hold this gathering?' I asked.

'Well, Merry Park would be the natural location,' he replied. 'But there's a bit of a swerve bias up there, and it probably wouldn't be deemed fair. Actually, I've had a word with Ray Coppin about using the Hospitality Room here, and he's given me the nod.'

I had to admit I was impressed with Bob's initiative. Not only had he conceived the idea of the meeting, but he'd already gone a long way to getting it organized.

Even so, it clearly wasn't going to happen overnight, as some of the invited delegates would be coming from distant parts of The Scheme. It was going to take a day or two to bring them all together. In the meantime, the Hospitality Room needed preparing, and Bob asked if I would be so kind as to get a start on that.

The room was down at the end of the main corridor, adjacent to the swing doors. It had been set aside for visiting dignitaries, which meant, basically, that it had a carpet instead of linoleum. There were no windows, but nonetheless a set of heavy velvet curtains hung where the windows would normally be. In the corner was a stack of leather-seated chairs and a large circular table. I found a vacuum cleaner in a small ante-room, gave the carpet a once-over, then moved the table and chairs into the middle. Bathing in the light of an electric chandelier, it now looked the perfect venue for a summit.

While I was getting all this done, I received occasional visits from curious passers-by. It seemed that word had spread about the forthcoming meeting, and now everyone wanted to offer advice and opinion.

'Tell Les Prentice from me,' said one driver, 'that the early swerve is non-negotiable.'

'You'll need ashtrays,' cautioned another. 'Lots of ashtrays.'

After about the tenth incursion by individuals who treated me either as a messenger boy, or as an unpaid butler, I closed up the Hospitality Room and locked the door. Something told me that the chosen representatives were in for a turbulent time, and I hoped I'd played a useful role in providing an atmosphere of sanctuary. When I saw Bob Little he told me the meeting was fixed for the following Monday at ten thirty.

That weekend the fine weather which had so far accompanied the strike broke at last, and by Monday morning it was raining lightly. As a result, every single one of the arriving delegates was wearing a mac, and as I watched them turn up it struck me how similar in appearance they all were. Les Prentice and John Ford I knew by sight, of course, but to tell the truth there was little to distinguish them from any of their colleagues. They were all typical Scheme men, and it was difficult to imagine that they held such strongly opposing views.

The swervers had come with a prepared Opening Statement, in which they proposed that early swerves should in future be built into the schedules, with a guaranteed three o'clock finish at least once a week. This was scoffed at by the flat-dayers, whose appointed spokesman described the proposal as 'illusory.'

His name was Andy Powell, and he was addressing a damp pre-summit assembly of supporters from beneath an umbrella. They were gathered in the vicinity of the vehicle wash, but because he was using the now-customary loud-hailer, his words could be clearly heard right across the yard.

'Sometimes,' he boomed, 'I think our friends the

swervers live in some kind of never-never land. They've never worked a full day, and what's more they never intend to!'

The accusation brought a round of harsh cheers from his audience, and thus encouraged he continued in a similar vein for several minutes more. By the time he'd finished he had run through the whole gamut of insults, gibes and insinuations, leaving the early swervers seething with indignation. Shortly afterwards they issued a Secondary Statement that described his comments as 'derisory' and 'unhelpful'.

It was in this uncompromising climate that fourteen chosen men were ushered into the Hospitality Room at ten thirty A.M.

'Nice start,' remarked Jonathan, as the door closed behind them.

The main corridor was crowded with onlookers keen to be first to hear the outcome of the meeting. As time passed, however, many of them drifted off to the canteen, eventually leaving just me, Jonathan and Bob Little, plus a few diehards. Not a sound could be heard from inside the room, and the rumpus we'd all expected appeared to have been avoided. Around one o'clock the door opened by two inches, and Bob was called over.

'Any progress?' I enquired, on his return.

'Not yet,' he replied. 'They've asked for beer and sandwiches to be sent in.'

'That's a good sign,' I said. 'At least they're being convivial.'

'Yes, well we got a case of beer in anticipation,' said

Bob. 'Do you think George can provide the sand-wiches?'

'I'll go and see,' said Jonathan, darting through the swing doors and up the canteen stairs. He was back in a jiffy. 'No he can't. He says he's far too busy.'

'Well, what are we going to do then?' Bob asked.

'Don't worry,' I said. 'I know just the man for the job.'

13

Martin's arrival, some forty minutes later, was like the appearance over the horizon of the cavalry. By this time the delegates had twice repeated their request for sustenance, and, according to Bob, were showing signs of increasing irritation. When, at last, he was able to assure them their sandwiches were being prepared, they settled down into a sort of expectant calm.

Martin had come equipped with a large basket containing all the necessary ingredients, as well as plates, knives and a breadboard. He set himself up in a room not too close to the canteen (so as not to aggravate George), and soon the sandwiches were being churned out thick and fast.

'Cheese and lettuce for the first round,' he announced. 'Followed by egg and cress if they require seconds.'

Each plateful was accompanied by a bottle of beer, and delivered personally into the Hospitality Room by Bob and Jonathan, who had now become Martin's eager assistant. I noticed that several not-so-helpful hangers-on had also shown up at about the same time as Martin. They hovered around his preparation table with the apparent hope of being fed, so that when Bob returned he was obliged to shoo them away in no uncertain terms.

'Blinking gannets,' he remarked. 'Got no shame at all, some people.'

Despite his gruffness, Bob was clearly pleased with the effect the refreshments were having on the representatives, and he encouraged Martin to cut a reserve supply of sandwiches for later in the afternoon. These were then covered with white napkins and placed under strict guard until required.

If anyone thought agreement would be easily reached, however, they were in for a disappointment. The men behind the closed doors may have been mellowed by their lunch-time treat, but collectively they were hard nuts to crack and in consequence the arguments persisted throughout the afternoon. Quite a few strikers went home at half past four, knowing that their fate was now in the hands of others. This left a hard core of swervers, flat-dayers and extremists, who kept sullen company together as evening arrived and the caterers began to clear up.

Martin had just finished packing everything into his basket when George paid him a visit.

'I've brought you a cup of tea,' he said. 'Expect no one else thought to get you one, did they?'

This was enough to overcome any potential rivalry which may have developed between the two of them, and within the space of ten minutes they were comparing notes on the best way to spread butter. Meanwhile, the meeting dragged on. The extra sandwiches were called for at six o'clock, along with further bottles of beer. When Bob took them in he made sure to inform the delegates that the cupboard was now bare. The idea was to try to speed them up a bit, but his efforts were of little avail. Not until some time after ten did the door open and a gaunt-looking John Ford emerge, followed by Andy Powell and the twelve others. They gathered in a group at the end of the corridor, then John and Andy stepped forward to make an address.

'It's been a difficult day,' John began. 'But thanks to the efforts of Bob and the rest of you we've managed to come to an accord. Both sides accept that a prolongation of the strike would achieve little, and therefore after much consideration we've prepared a Joint Statement which my colleague will now read out.'

There was a pause while Andy Powell slowly unfolded a sheet of paper he'd been clutching in his left hand. One or two onlookers shuffled their feet in anticipation. Others cleared their throats on Andy's behalf. Then he held the statement before him and read aloud:

'We're unanimous that the principle of the flat-day should be adhered to, but that early swerves can be granted if and when circumstances dictate.'

Another pause followed.

'Is that it?' someone asked.

'Yep,' Andy replied. 'That's it.'

'What about the ten-off-the-eight?'

'The ten-off-the-eight still stands.'

This brought a general cheer, and the fourteen delegates then indulged in a long round of hand-shaking, back-patting and mutual self-congratulation.

'In other words,' murmured George. 'We're back to where we were in the first place.'

The return to work was a dignified affair. On Wednesday morning, after a day of 'consultation and agreement', the entire staff clocked in as though there had never been a strike. Then, at half past eight, a column of UniVans headed out through the gate, led by a vehicle bedecked with pennants. Warehousemen of both persuasions watched from the loading bay and combined to give them a rousing send-off. In this way they signalled that the conflict was well and truly over.

Even so, the reappearance of UniVans on the roads and streets didn't have quite the effect most of us expected. It had been widely assumed that the end of the dispute would be welcomed by the populace at large. George and I were surprised, therefore, by the number of funny looks we received as we began our journey along the Ring Road. We lost count of the amount of times people glanced at us and then shook their heads with disdain, as if to say, 'What a disgrace going on strike like that!'

Meanwhile, our fellow motorists seemed less forgiving of UniVans than they had been in the past, and indeed some were downright obstructive. At first I thought they simply begrudged giving up the road space they'd enjoyed during our period of idleness, which was fair enough. After having been deliberately carved up for the fifth time, however, I realized there was a degree of malice in the action.

'What's the matter with everyone?' asked George, as a car overtook us, and then braked to turn left.

'We appear to have lost our popularity,' I replied.

'But we've just endured a three week strike in order to safeguard The Scheme!' he protested.

'That's not how the public see it.'

Fortunately, the sheer volume of the operation meant that UniVans soon held sway on the roads again. By early-afternoon the harassment had fizzled out and we'd begun to merge back into the fabric of daily life. Nonetheless, it was a relief finally to turn off the Ring Road and head in a new direction. The revised schedules were now in place, and our latest duty included a run to Eden Lacy. With the weather brightening, we cruised merrily along as I pointed out the various landmarks I'd noted during my days on the timing run.

Yet although George paid some heed to the location of certain pull-ins and cafes, it soon became clear that his chief interest lay in his forthcoming meeting with Martin. He was eager to see him operating on his home turf, as it were, having been most impressed by the sandwiches he'd produced. I had a feeling George was more concerned with Martin's methods than the ingredients he used, but even so I was pleased to share his sense of anticipation as we approached the entrance to Eden Lacy depot. The place looked quieter than ever, and at first sight appeared totally unaffected by the imposition of the new schedules. Then I noticed that standing on the bay talking to Harold, Martin and Eric was a super in a smart, new uniform. We drew up in the yard to be met by Steve Moore, freshly promoted and looking most satisfied with life.

'You kept that quiet,' I remarked, as I got out of the cab.

'Thought I'd better,' he replied. 'Didn't want to make anyone jealous, did I?'

'You here full time?'

'Yep,' he said. 'The first superintendent to be permanently attached to Eden Lacy.'

I looked at his silver badge, glinting in the sunshine, and realized that life for Harold and the others would never be quite the same again. The office door that had been locked for so long now stood open and ready for Steve to begin his tenure. This meant, for the time being at least, that there'd be no more languid games of cards, lasting for hours on end. The card table had already been discreetly folded away, and the three warehousemen were occupying themselves by giving the floor a sweep. Then Harold boarded the forklift and came to unload us.

'We haven't stopped all day,' he said. 'There's been a van here every twenty minutes.'

'Well, at least you're on the map now,' I replied. 'What's Steve Moore been like?'

'He's a bit zealous to tell you the truth. Keeps marching round checking on everything.'

'Oh dear.'

'Not to worry,' said Harold. 'We'll soon have him softened up with tea and sandwiches.'

The very schemishness of this remark suggested that, despite the change in circumstances, all was well at Eden Lacy. As usual, Eric was wandering around with a big smile on his face, and I had no doubt that over in the engineer's shop Jim would be whistling while he worked. Meanwhile, George and Martin were engaged deep in conversation on their favourite subject.

'I prefer a diagonal sandwich where possible,' Martin was saying. 'Although the square cut is better for lunch boxes.'

'Medium sliced?' George enquired.

'Where possible, yes.'

'And would salt be optional?'

'Naturally.'

The arrival in the yard of another UniVan interrupted their discourse, but all the same I could see that a new friendship was burgeoning. Over the coming days I would get quite used to hearing talk of bread knives, cheese slicers and the crispness of lettuce, as if the two of them were aiming to revolutionize the catering trade. Whether they'd actually do anything about it was an entirely different matter. The idea of leaving The Scheme, with all its safeguards, and venturing into the world outside, was unthinkable to most employees. I could barely remember half a dozen people who'd made such a move, and in each case they'd returned to the fold after a few months. Nevertheless, the pair continued with their optimistic plans. Within a week George had made contact with Sandro and reestablished the cake run. Not long after that he took Martin home to meet Trace, and they all looked set to live happily ever after.

On the morning of the 1st of June, Bob Little called me over to his counter and told me not to bother clocking in.

'Got a special duty for you today,' he said. 'It's the annual weight test and they need an empty van delivering.'

'Oh, right.'

'Do you know where the weighbridge is?'

'Yep.'

'OK then,' said Bob. 'There'll be a few officials present, so you'd better take George along with you.'

The test wasn't until eleven o'clock, which gave us time to enjoy a leisurely breakfast before we collected the keys for UV55 and set off. We arrived with ten minutes to spare.

'Looks like quite an occasion,' George remarked.

There were about fifteen people attending the ceremony, and I saw straightaway that they were divided into three distinct groups. The first consisted of assorted depot managers, including Ray Coppin, who gave me a nod of recognition when we pulled up. These managers all looked roughly the same, wearing the same kind of crumpled suits, and they stood around laughing at each other's jokes. A short distance away was the second group: the superintendents, all in full uniform. Nesbitt was there, of course, and beside him stood a tall, thin man whom I took to be Scapens. They were accompanied by a handful of lower-order supers, including Horsefall. He was clearly delighted to be taking part in such an important event, and as he rubbed shoulders with his Gold Badge superiors we could almost see his tail wagging.

Also present was Joyce. She was standing not with her fellow supers, but amongst the third group: a cluster of slick-looking individuals that I wouldn't normally have associated with The Scheme. There were five of them in all, and they each carried a glossy black attaché case, and paid no attention to anyone outside their immediate circle. Surprisingly enough, Joyce appeared completely at ease in their company, and as I gazed at her it struck me that she seemed taller than I remembered. Then I noticed that instead of her usual sensible black shoes, she was today wearing high-heeled boots. She was engaged in deep conversation with the others, and at one point she removed her peaked cap, causing her hair to tumble around her shoulders. She looked magnificent, and at that moment I realized the future belonged to people like her.

The man in charge of the weighbridge, by contrast, had Scheme stamped all over him. After taking ages to emerge from his hut, he then fussed self-importantly round the mechanism as if he were about to weigh gold dust at some oriental bazaar, rather than just a common or garden UniVan. On his instructions I drove onto a large iron plate, then George and I got out of the cab and walked round to watch proceedings from a polite distance.

There was little possibility of seeing the details of what was going on, however, as the more important witnesses had already gathered in front of the indicator gauge, thereby obscuring it from view.

After a long delay George said, 'They seem to be taking a long time. Is it coin-operated or something?'

'Don't know,' I replied. 'Maybe it's not working properly.'

As if to confirm this, one of the supers came over and asked me to reverse the van off the weighbridge, then back on again. I did as he asked, then rejoined George. By now there was a lot of head-shaking and murmuring going on, and the only people who looked pleased with the outcome were those grouped around Joyce. The rest appeared slightly downcast, and I noticed that Horsefall's imaginary tail had ceased wagging.

Finally, we were approached by Nesbitt. 'Alright, thank you lads,' he said. 'You can go and have your dinner now. Expect you're both quite peckish, aren't you?'

'Yes.'

'Well, off you go then. And make the most of it.'

We got back into the van, started up, and trundled off the weighbridge. The official party remained where it was, all eyes on us as we departed.

On the way home a thought occurred to me.

'You know that pallet trolley we've been carrying round for weeks?'

'Yeah?' replied George.

'Do you think it could have made any difference to the weight test?'

'Shouldn't think so,' he said. 'One of Trace's cakes maybe, but not that trolley.'

I was on The Scheme for five years, three months and four days. I know this because a fortnight after the weight test I received a letter telling me as much. It also informed me that because the test had been failed The Scheme would have to be wound down over the coming months.

'In other words, they've pulled the plug,' said George, who'd received an identical letter, except that he'd only done two years. 'Quite handy really.'

'Handy?' I said. 'How come?'

'I'll get two years' worth of redundancy, won't I? Just right if you're starting up a business.'

So George, at least, was happy. And Martin as well. Which just left the rest of us. General consensus was that the people at the top had simply been looking for an excuse to close us down, and the weight test had done the trick perfectly.

The letter went on to say that, in any case, the national mood had swung round. There was no longer any public support for a Scheme that produced nothing, and the buildings and capital would be better used if sold off to the private sector. The letter was signed by a Miss J. Meredith.

Resistance, of course, was futile. Over the following days several mass meetings took place at which calls were made for immediate industrial action. Unfortunately, as we'd discovered during the strike, we wielded no economic clout. Therefore such measures would be of little effect. Besides, hostile voices were soon heard saying that employees on The Scheme had had it far too easy for far too long, and that we'd finally got what was coming to us. The times had changed, they said, and the quicker we accepted this the better.

When the enthusiasts found out what was happening they launched a campaign called Save The UniVan. At long last they made direct contact with the workforce and some talks were held, but nothing came of them. Then, when the enthusiasts realised they'd probably be able to buy unwanted vans for discount prices, they suddenly quietened down. In due course a couple of hundred vehicles were put on the open market, and the higher-quality models were snapped up at once.

All the same, a huge surplus remained. These were

ferried over to Merry Park, which had now become an elephant's graveyard for UniVans. They stood in silent lines, rank after rank, watched over by John Jones (who'd somehow managed to retain his job in the gate-house). A few of the other depots were bought by property developers. Most, though, were of no use for anything. Long Reach was shut down in the last days of September, by which time weeds and small saplings had begun to emerge through the cracks in the concrete.

As for the staff, well we all got a bit of money. Not much, but enough to stop us moaning. Even so, the swiftness of the closures had come as a profound shock. No one expected The Scheme to collapse overnight. We really thought that it would go on and on for ever, a procession of UniVans leading the way into a bright and promising future. Instead, we squandered everything with our petty bickering, our inertia, and our stubbornness. Then we watched helpless as the whole vast edifice was dismantled before our eyes. We'd been warned and we'd taken no notice. Now all was lost. The cold winds were returning. It was the end of our glorious summer.

DEPARTMENT OF SUPERINTENDENTS

Gold Badge

Breslin	Scapens
Nesbitt	Wilkin

Silver Badge

Askew	Hackett
Atkinson	Harris
Bamford	Hogg
Bland	Horlick
Booth	Horsefall
Charnock	Hoskins
Collis	Huggins
Cowan	Knapp
Crowe	McCabe
Dawson	Meeks
Gosling	Mercer

Meredith	Smart
Moody	Spender
Osgood	Strickland
Podmore	Trant
Pick	Warren
Sedgefield	Watts